Cassandra

ANIMAL PSYCHIC

#1

CASSANDRA STEPS OUT

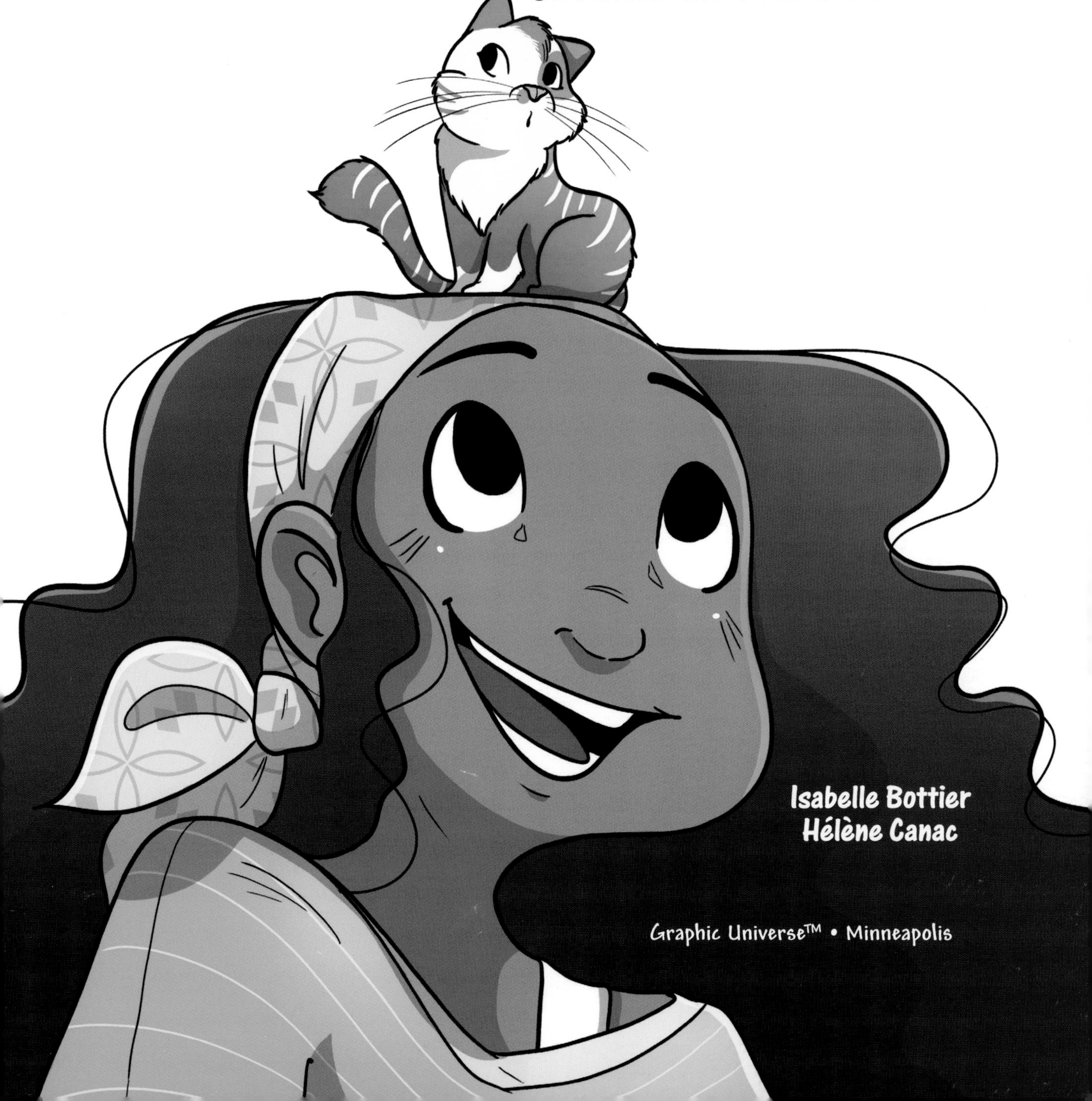

Isabelle Bottier
Hélène Canac

Graphic Universe™ • Minneapolis

A huge thank-you to Estelle and Isabelle for this project, which fits me 100 percent! It's such a pleasure to work with you! Thanks also for my Choupi for encouraging me during the creation of this volume and to Agnes for making Juliet's bedroom so wonderfully beautiful. Victor, Daphne, Martin, this album is for you . . . once you can read!

—H.C.

A big thank-you to Estelle for her kindness and to Hélène for creating such a lovely Cassandra. And a big treat to the real Dolly, who continues to live in the heart of her master.

—I.B.

Story by Isabelle Bottier
Illustrations by Hélène Canac
Coloring by Drac

First American edition published in 2019 by Graphic Universe™

Published by arrangement with Steinkis Groupe

Cassandra prend son envol © 2017 by Jungle

Translation by Norwyn MacTire

English translation copyright © 2019 by Lerner Publishing Group, Inc.

Graphic Universe™ is a trademark of Lerner Publishing Group, Inc.

Graphic Universe™
A division of Lerner Publishing Group, Inc.
241 First Avenue North
Minneapolis, MN 55401 USA

For reading levels and more information, look up this title at www.lernerbooks.com.

Main body text set in Andy Std 9/10.5.
Typeface provided by Monotype Typography.

Library of Congress Cataloging-in-Publication Data

Names: Bottier, Isabelle, author. | Canac, Hélène, illustrator. | MacTyre, Norwyn, translator.
Title: Cassandra steps out / Isabelle Bottier ; Helene Canac ; coloring by Drac ; translation by Norwyn MacTyre.
Other titles: Cassandra prend son envol. French.
Description: First American edition. | Minneapolis : Graphic Universe, 2019. | Series: Cassandra, animal psychic ; book 1 | Summary: While struggling to cope with major changes in her life, fourteen-year-old Cassandra decides to help others by using her ability to see what animals are thinking, beginning with finding a lost cat.
Identifiers: LCCN 2018052142 (print) | LCCN 2018056241 (ebook) | ISBN 9781541561106 (eb pdf) | ISBN 9781541543973 (lb : alk. paper) | ISBN 9781541572836 (pb : alk. paper)
Subjects: LCSH: Graphic novels. | CYAC: Graphic novels. | Psychic ability—Fiction. | Human-animal communication—Fiction. | Change (Psychology)—Fiction. | Family life—Fiction.
Classification: LCC PZ7.7.B675 (ebook) | LCC PZ7.7.B675 Cas 2019 (print) | DDC 741.5/944—dc23

LC record available at https://lccn.loc.gov/2018052142

Manufactured in the United States of America
1-45426-39683-2/8/2019

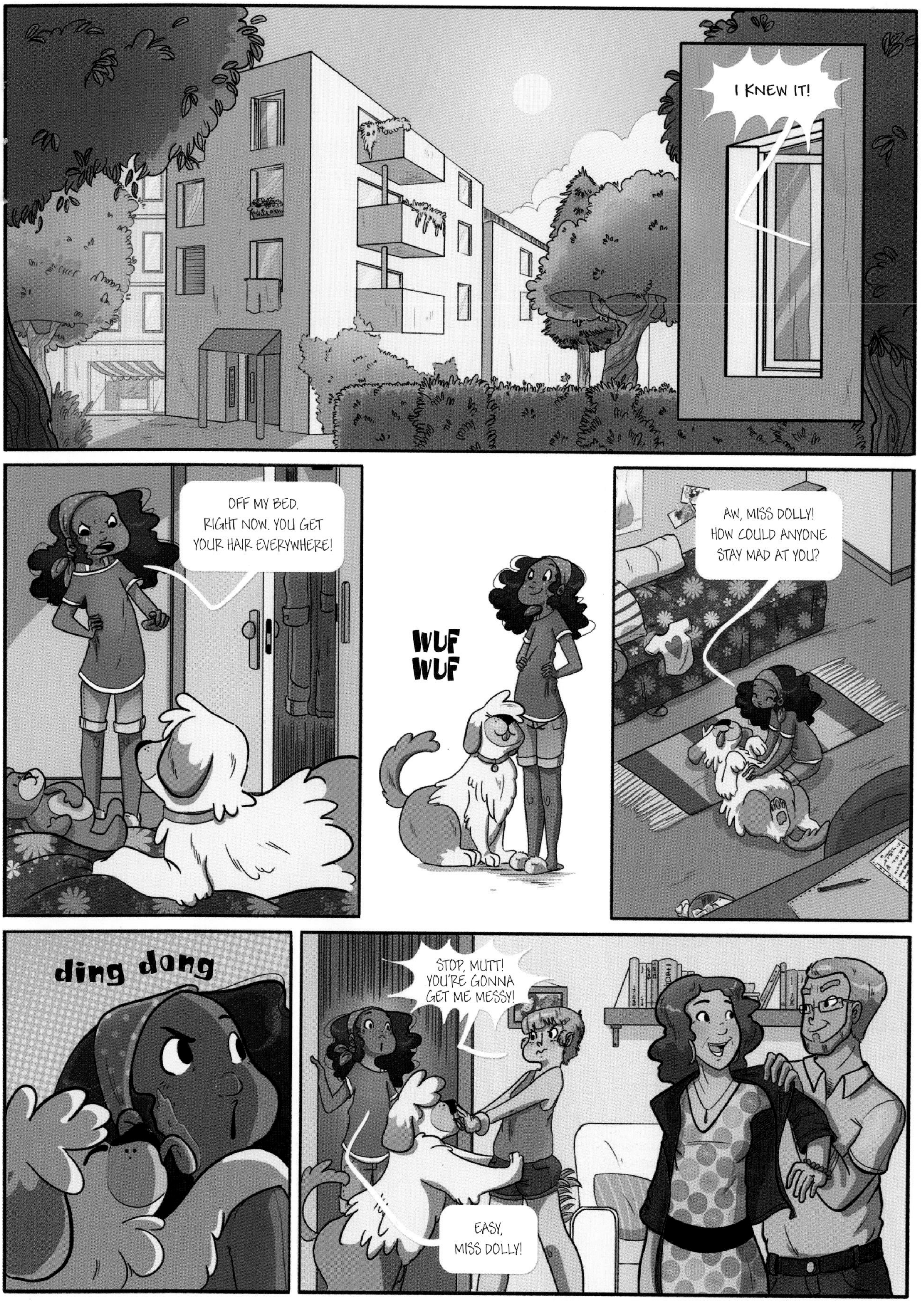
I KNEW IT!
OFF MY BED. RIGHT NOW. YOU GET YOUR HAIR EVERYWHERE!
WUF WUF
AW, MISS DOLLY! HOW COULD ANYONE STAY MAD AT YOU?
ding dong
STOP, MUTT! YOU'RE GONNA GET ME MESSY!
EASY, MISS DOLLY!

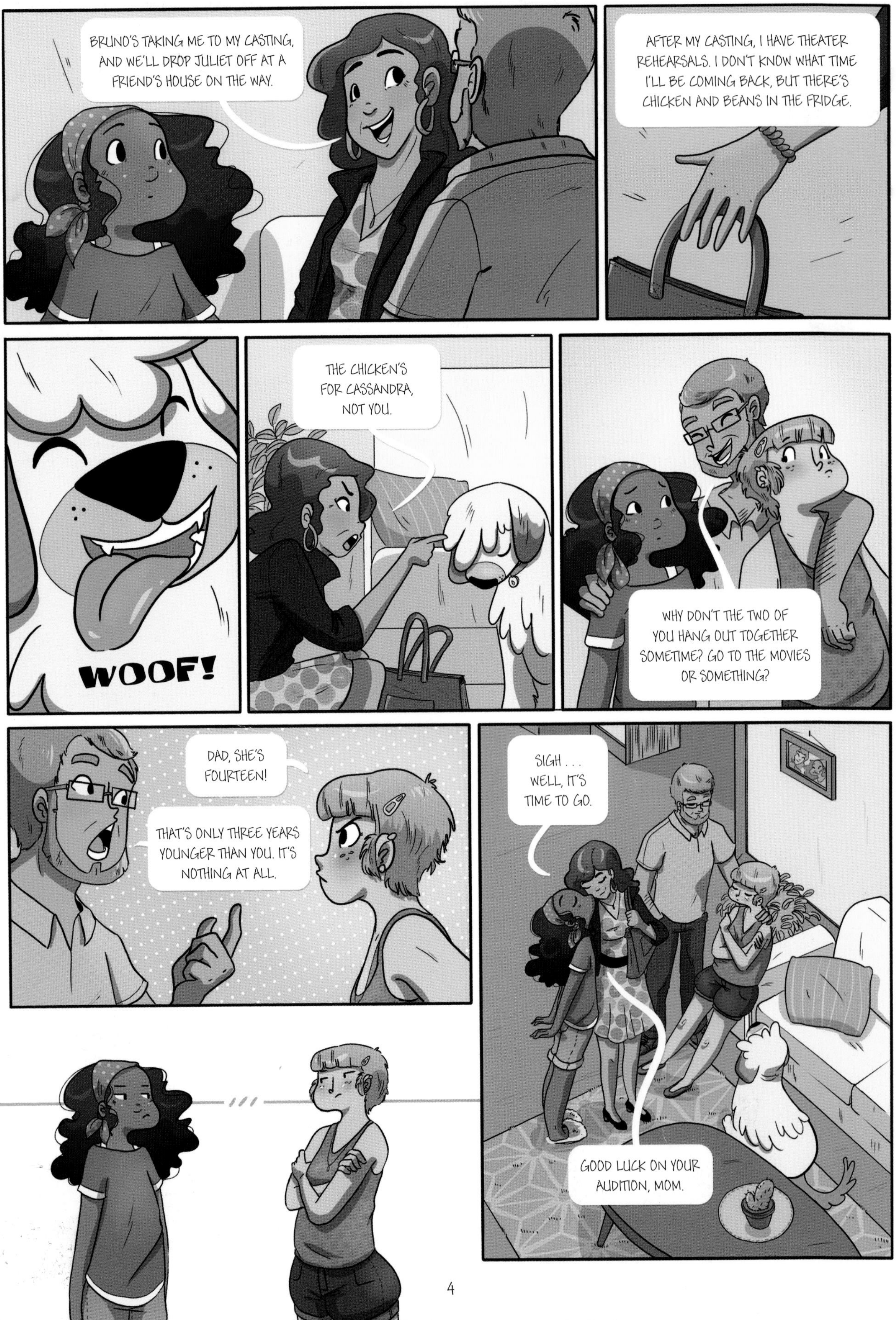
BRUNO'S TAKING ME TO MY CASTING, AND WE'LL DROP JULIET OFF AT A FRIEND'S HOUSE ON THE WAY.
AFTER MY CASTING, I HAVE THEATER REHEARSALS. I DON'T KNOW WHAT TIME I'LL BE COMING BACK, BUT THERE'S CHICKEN AND BEANS IN THE FRIDGE.
WOOF!
THE CHICKEN'S FOR CASSANDRA, NOT YOU.
WHY DON'T THE TWO OF YOU HANG OUT TOGETHER SOMETIME? GO TO THE MOVIES OR SOMETHING?
DAD, SHE'S FOURTEEN!
THAT'S ONLY THREE YEARS YOUNGER THAN YOU. IT'S NOTHING AT ALL.
SIGH . . . WELL, IT'S TIME TO GO.
GOOD LUCK ON YOUR AUDITION, MOM.

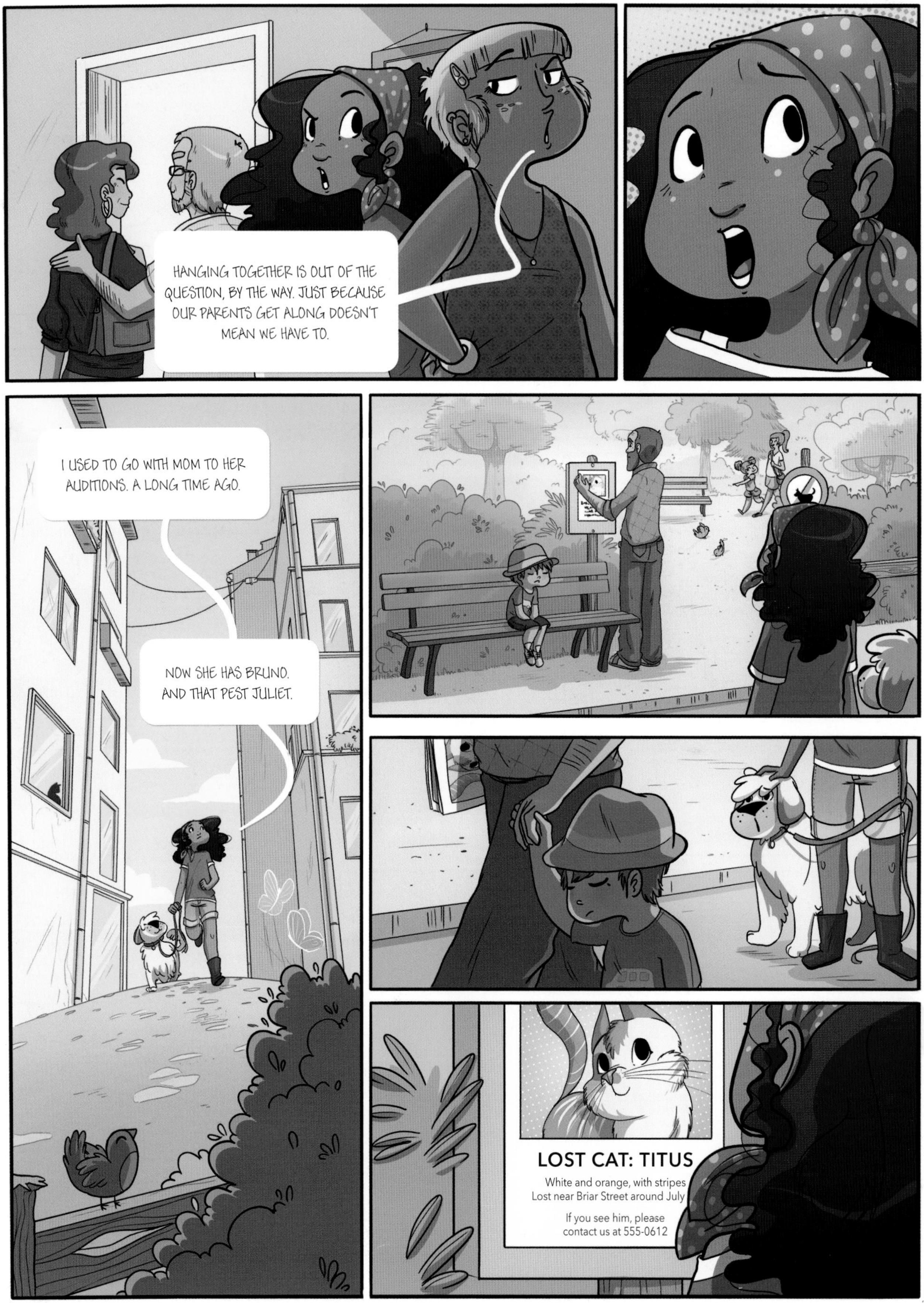
HANGING TOGETHER IS OUT OF THE QUESTION, BY THE WAY. JUST BECAUSE OUR PARENTS GET ALONG DOESN'T MEAN WE HAVE TO.
I USED TO GO WITH MOM TO HER AUDITIONS. A LONG TIME AGO.
NOW SHE HAS BRUNO. AND THAT PEST JULIET.
LOST CAT: TITUS
White and orange, with stripes
Lost near Briar Street around July
If you see him, please
contact us at 555-0612

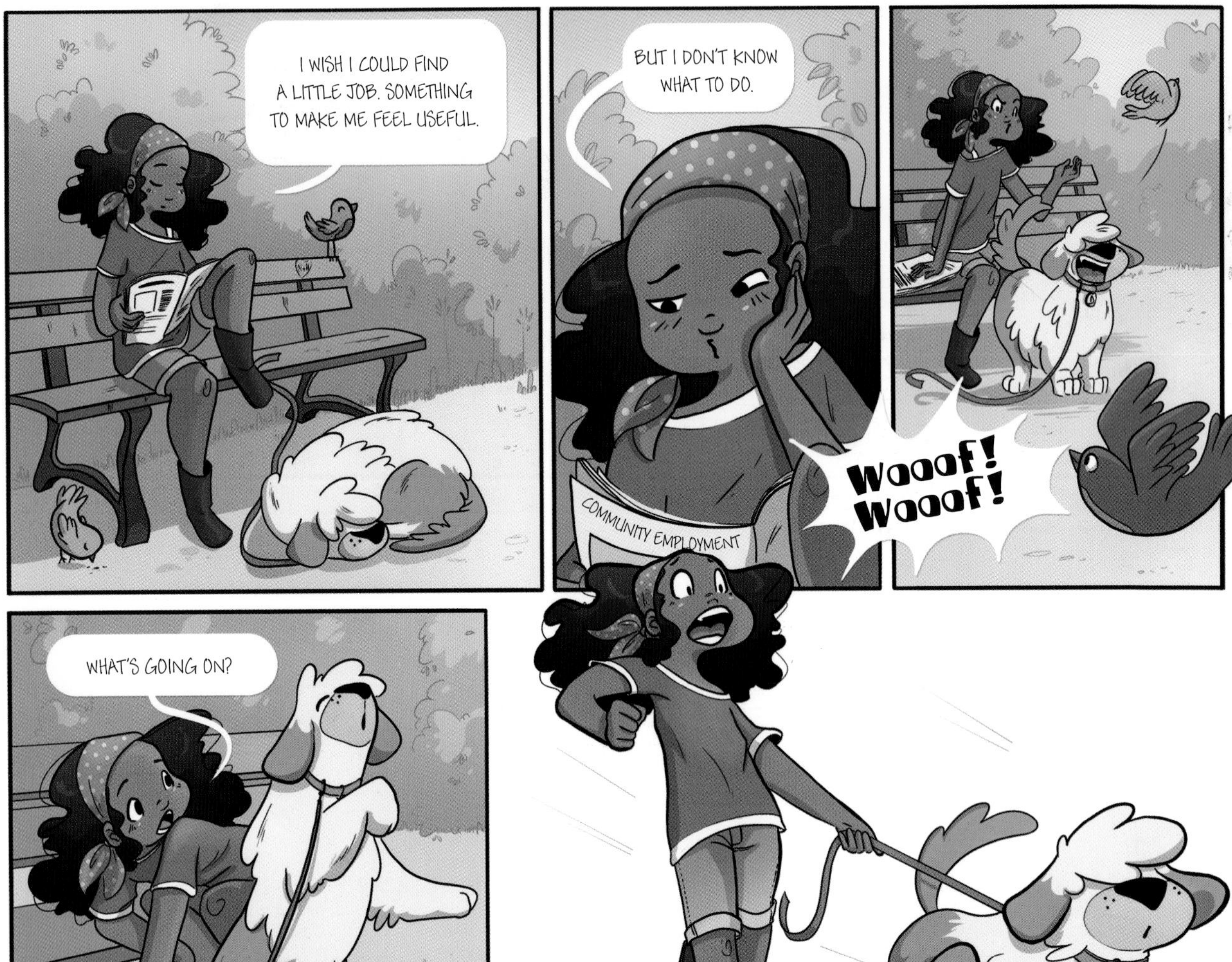
I WISH I COULD FIND A LITTLE JOB. SOMETHING TO MAKE ME FEEL USEFUL.
BUT I DON'T KNOW WHAT TO DO.
COMMUNITY EMPLOYMENT
Wooof! Wooof!
WHAT'S GOING ON?
Wooof!
3004MD16
OH! WHAT ARE **YOU** DOING ALL ALONE?

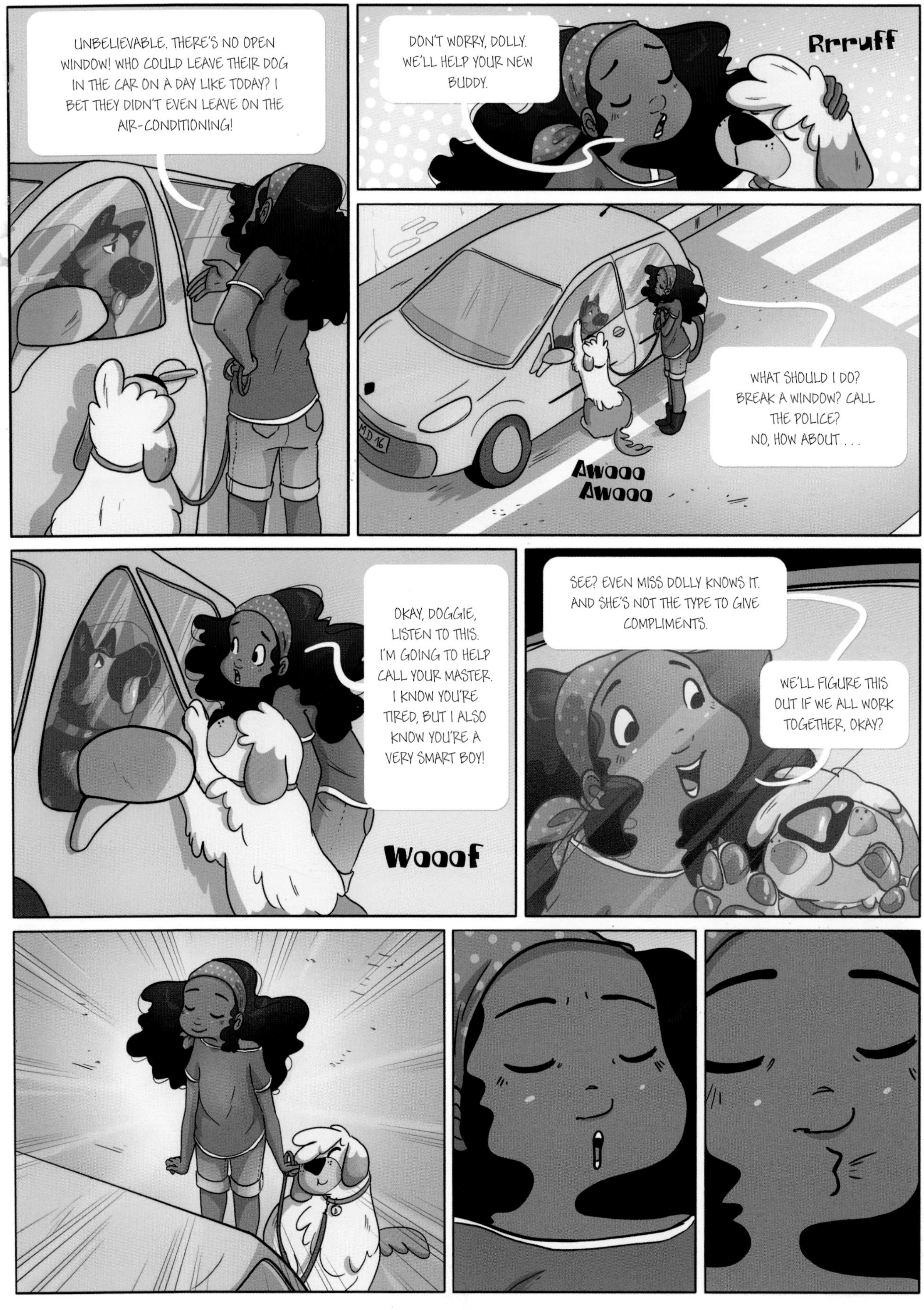
UNBELIEVABLE. THERE'S NO OPEN WINDOW! WHO COULD LEAVE THEIR DOG IN THE CAR ON A DAY LIKE TODAY? I BET THEY DIDN'T EVEN LEAVE ON THE AIR-CONDITIONING!
DON'T WORRY, DOLLY. WE'LL HELP YOUR NEW BUDDY.
Rrruff
MD 16
Awooo
Awooo
WHAT SHOULD I DO? BREAK A WINDOW? CALL THE POLICE? NO, HOW ABOUT . . .
OKAY, DOGGIE, LISTEN TO THIS. I'M GOING TO HELP CALL YOUR MASTER. I KNOW YOU'RE TIRED, BUT I ALSO KNOW YOU'RE A VERY SMART BOY!
Wooof
SEE? EVEN MISS DOLLY KNOWS IT. AND SHE'S NOT THE TYPE TO GIVE COMPLIMENTS.
WE'LL FIGURE THIS OUT IF WE ALL WORK TOGETHER, OKAY?

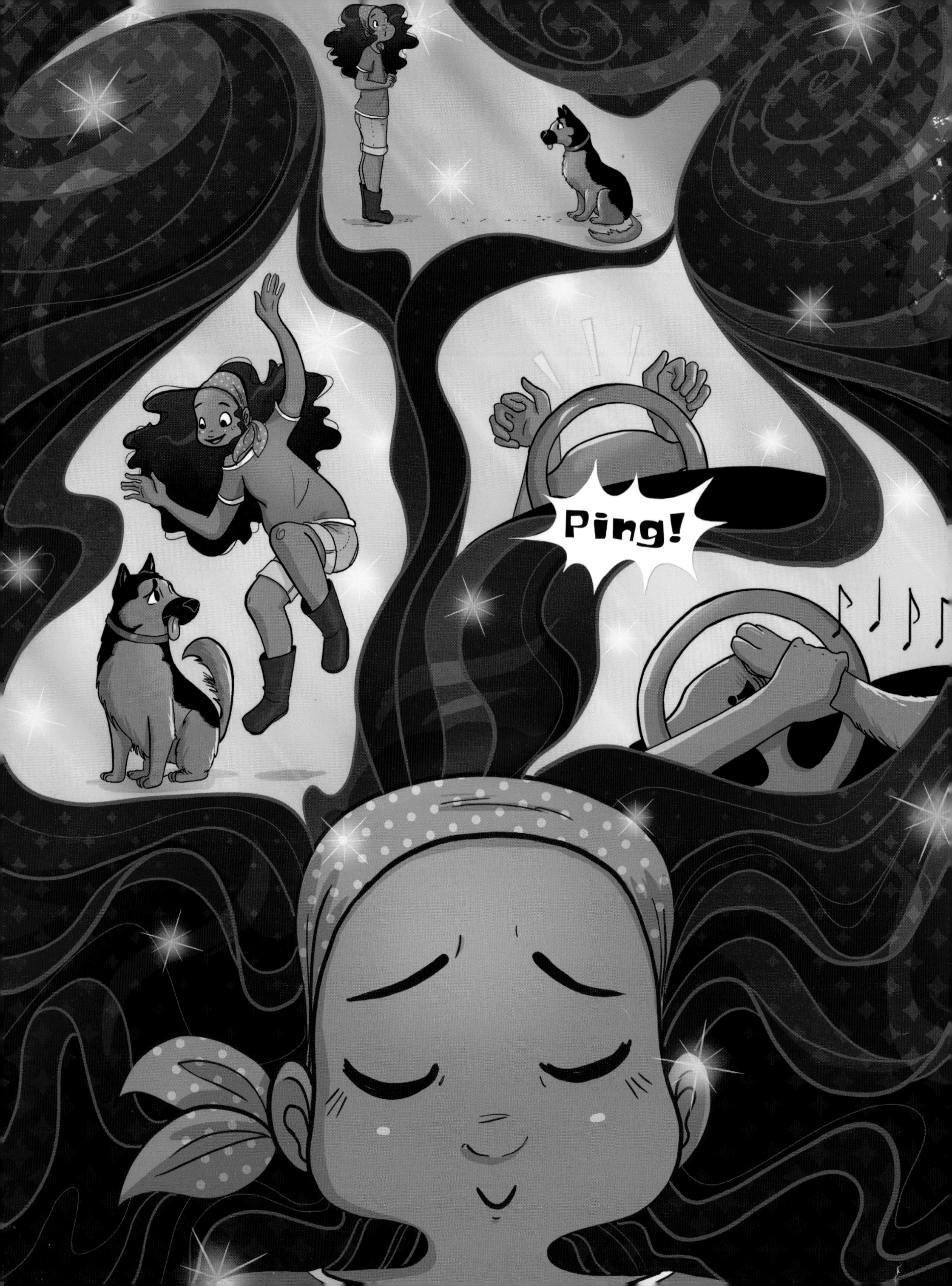
Ping!

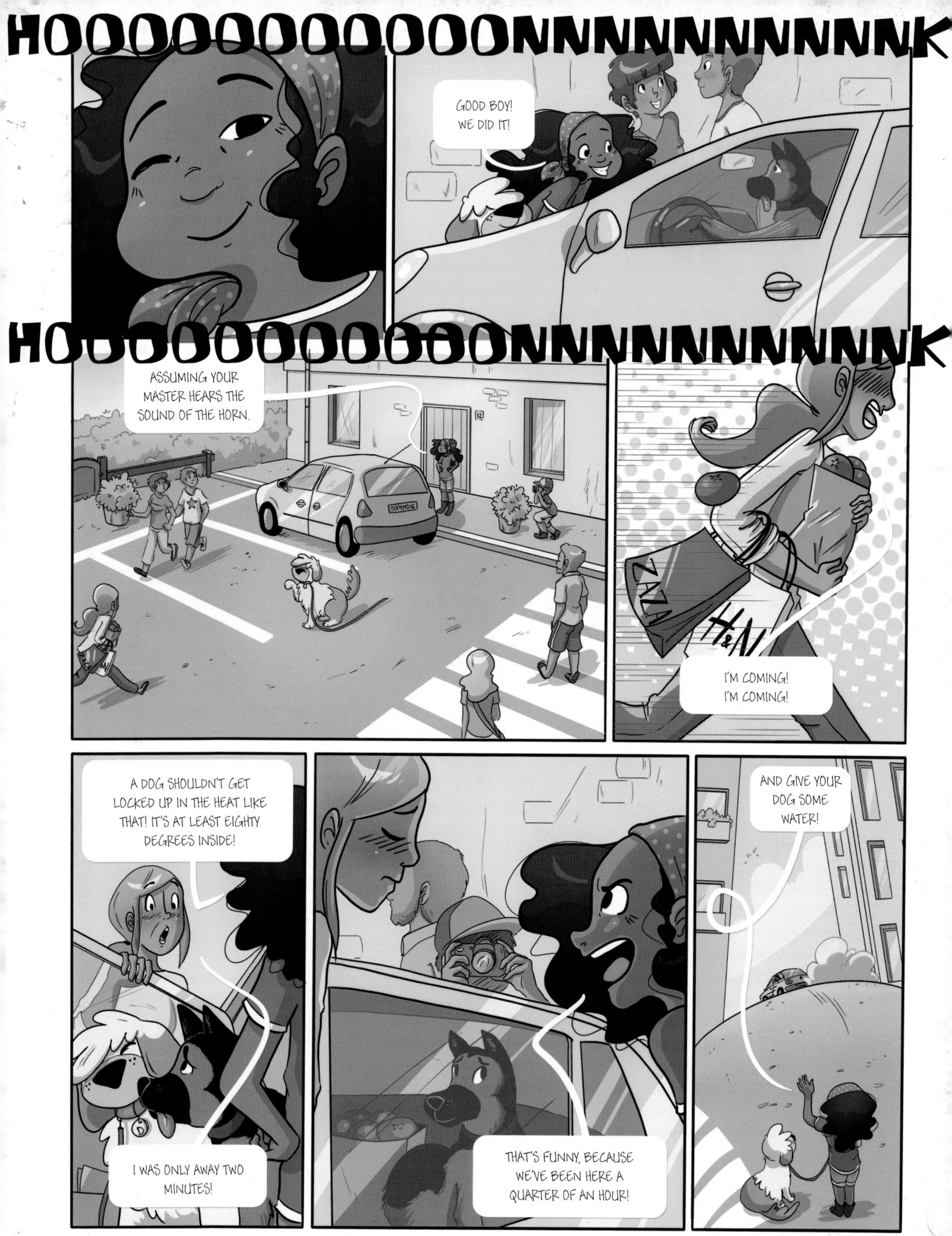
HOOOOOOOOOOOONNNNNNNNNNK
GOOD BOY! WE DID IT!
HOOOOOOOOOOOONNNNNNNNNNK
ASSUMING YOUR MASTER HEARS THE SOUND OF THE HORN.
I'M COMING! I'M COMING!
A DOG SHOULDN'T GET LOCKED UP IN THE HEAT LIKE THAT! IT'S AT LEAST EIGHTY DEGREES INSIDE!
I WAS ONLY AWAY TWO MINUTES!
THAT'S FUNNY, BECAUSE WE'VE BEEN HERE A QUARTER OF AN HOUR!
AND GIVE YOUR DOG SOME WATER!

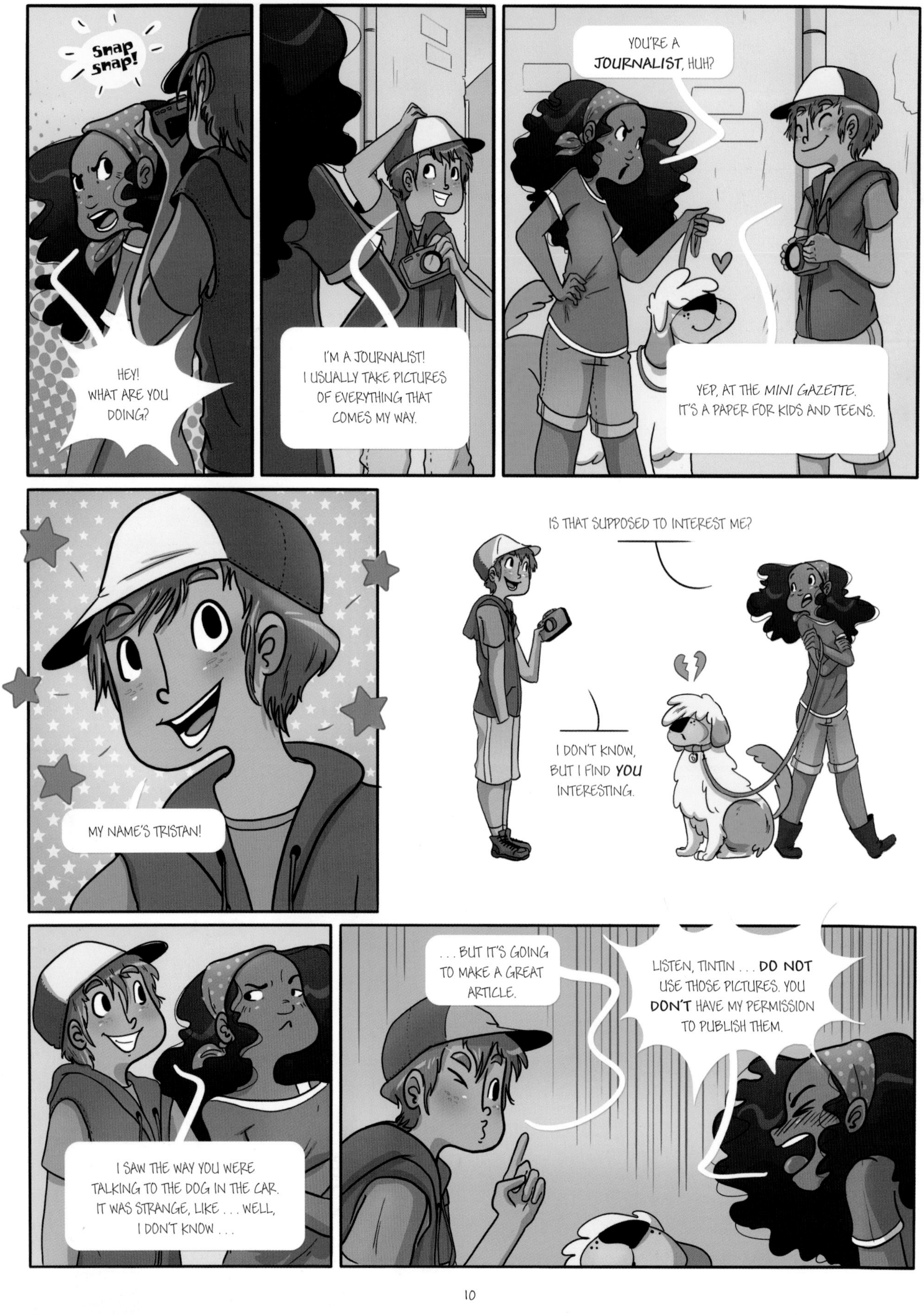
Snap snap!
HEY! WHAT ARE YOU DOING?
I'M A JOURNALIST! I USUALLY TAKE PICTURES OF EVERYTHING THAT COMES MY WAY.
YOU'RE A **JOURNALIST**, HUH?
YEP, AT THE *MINI GAZETTE*. IT'S A PAPER FOR KIDS AND TEENS.
MY NAME'S TRISTAN!
IS THAT SUPPOSED TO INTEREST ME?
I DON'T KNOW, BUT I FIND **YOU** INTERESTING.
I SAW THE WAY YOU WERE TALKING TO THE DOG IN THE CAR. IT WAS STRANGE, LIKE . . . WELL, I DON'T KNOW . . .
. . . BUT IT'S GOING TO MAKE A GREAT ARTICLE.
LISTEN, TINTIN . . . **DO NOT** USE THOSE PICTURES. YOU **DON'T** HAVE MY PERMISSION TO PUBLISH THEM.

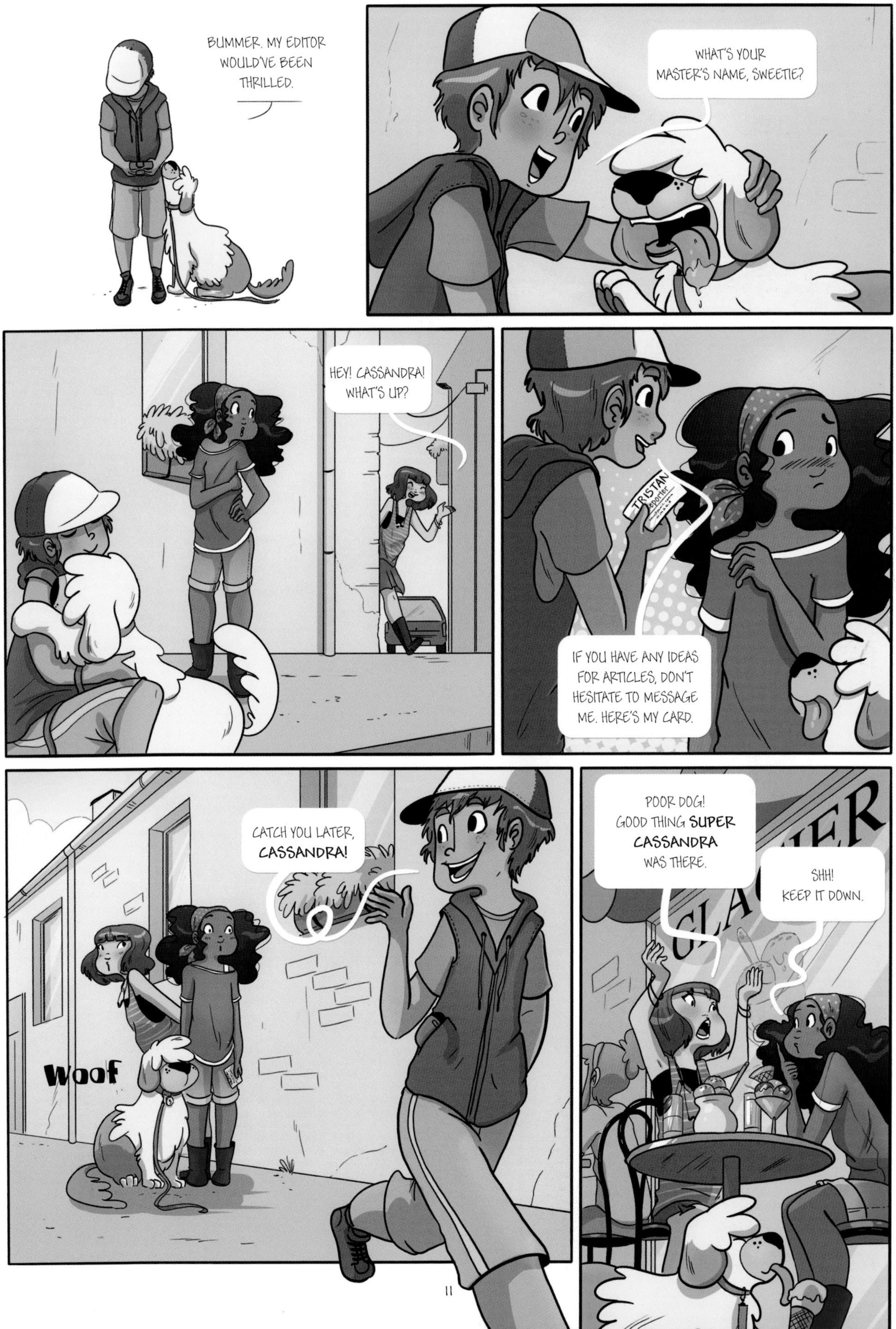
BUMMER. MY EDITOR WOULD'VE BEEN THRILLED.
WHAT'S YOUR MASTER'S NAME, SWEETIE?
HEY! CASSANDRA! WHAT'S UP?
TRISTAN
reporter
IF YOU HAVE ANY IDEAS FOR ARTICLES, DON'T HESITATE TO MESSAGE ME. HERE'S MY CARD.
CATCH YOU LATER, **CASSANDRA!**
WOOF
POOR DOG! GOOD THING **SUPER CASSANDRA** WAS THERE.
SHH! KEEP IT DOWN.

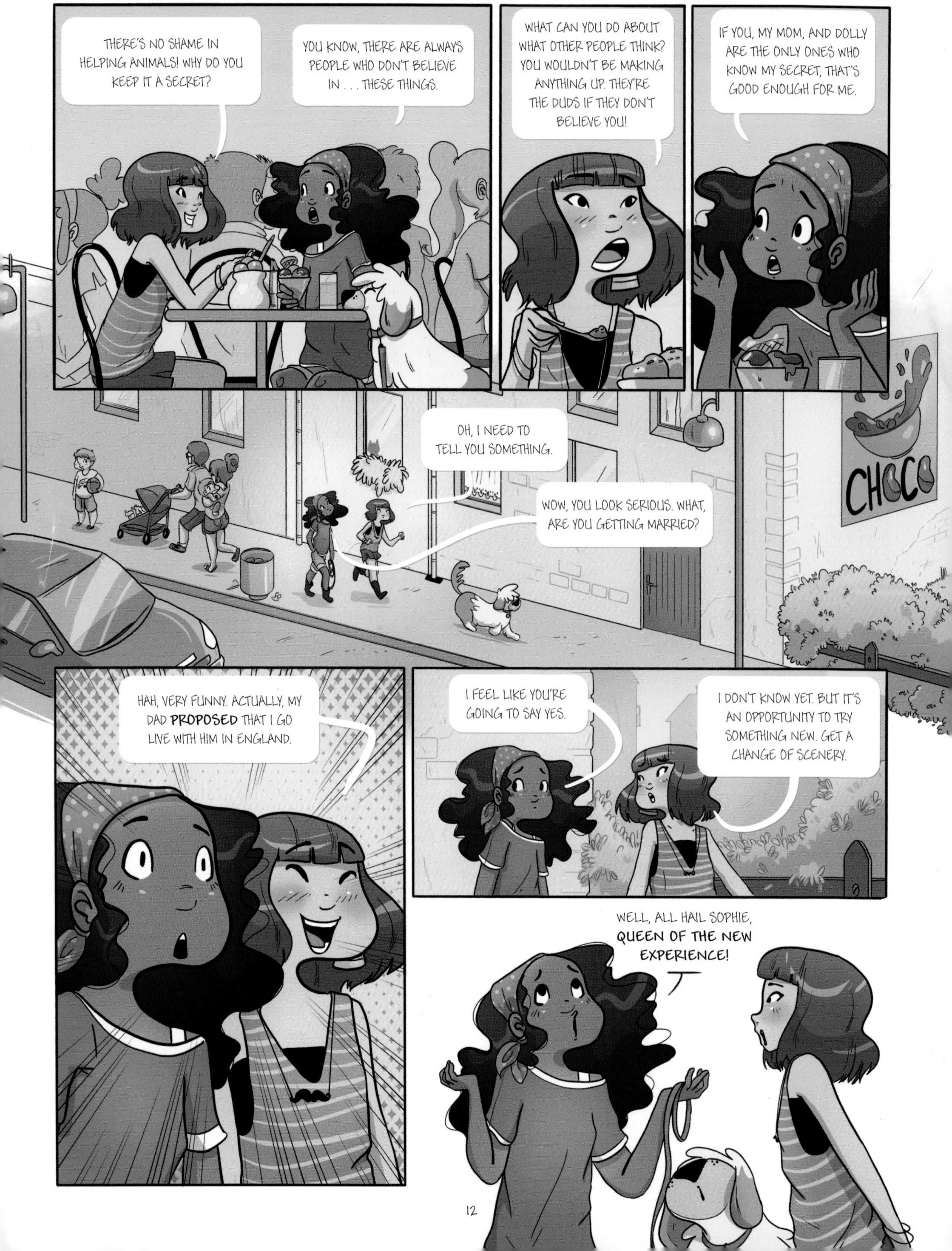

THERE'S NO SHAME IN HELPING ANIMALS! WHY DO YOU KEEP IT A SECRET?
YOU KNOW, THERE ARE ALWAYS PEOPLE WHO DON'T BELIEVE IN . . . THESE THINGS.
WHAT CAN YOU DO ABOUT WHAT OTHER PEOPLE THINK? YOU WOULDN'T BE MAKING ANYTHING UP. THEY'RE THE DUDS IF THEY DON'T BELIEVE YOU!
IF YOU, MY MOM, AND DOLLY ARE THE ONLY ONES WHO KNOW MY SECRET, THAT'S GOOD ENOUGH FOR ME.
OH, I NEED TO TELL YOU SOMETHING.
WOW, YOU LOOK SERIOUS. WHAT, ARE YOU GETTING MARRIED?
CHOCO
HAH, VERY FUNNY. ACTUALLY, MY DAD **PROPOSED** THAT I GO LIVE WITH HIM IN ENGLAND.
I FEEL LIKE YOU'RE GOING TO SAY YES.
I DON'T KNOW YET. BUT IT'S AN OPPORTUNITY TO TRY SOMETHING NEW. GET A CHANGE OF SCENERY.
WELL, ALL HAIL SOPHIE, **QUEEN OF THE NEW EXPERIENCE!**

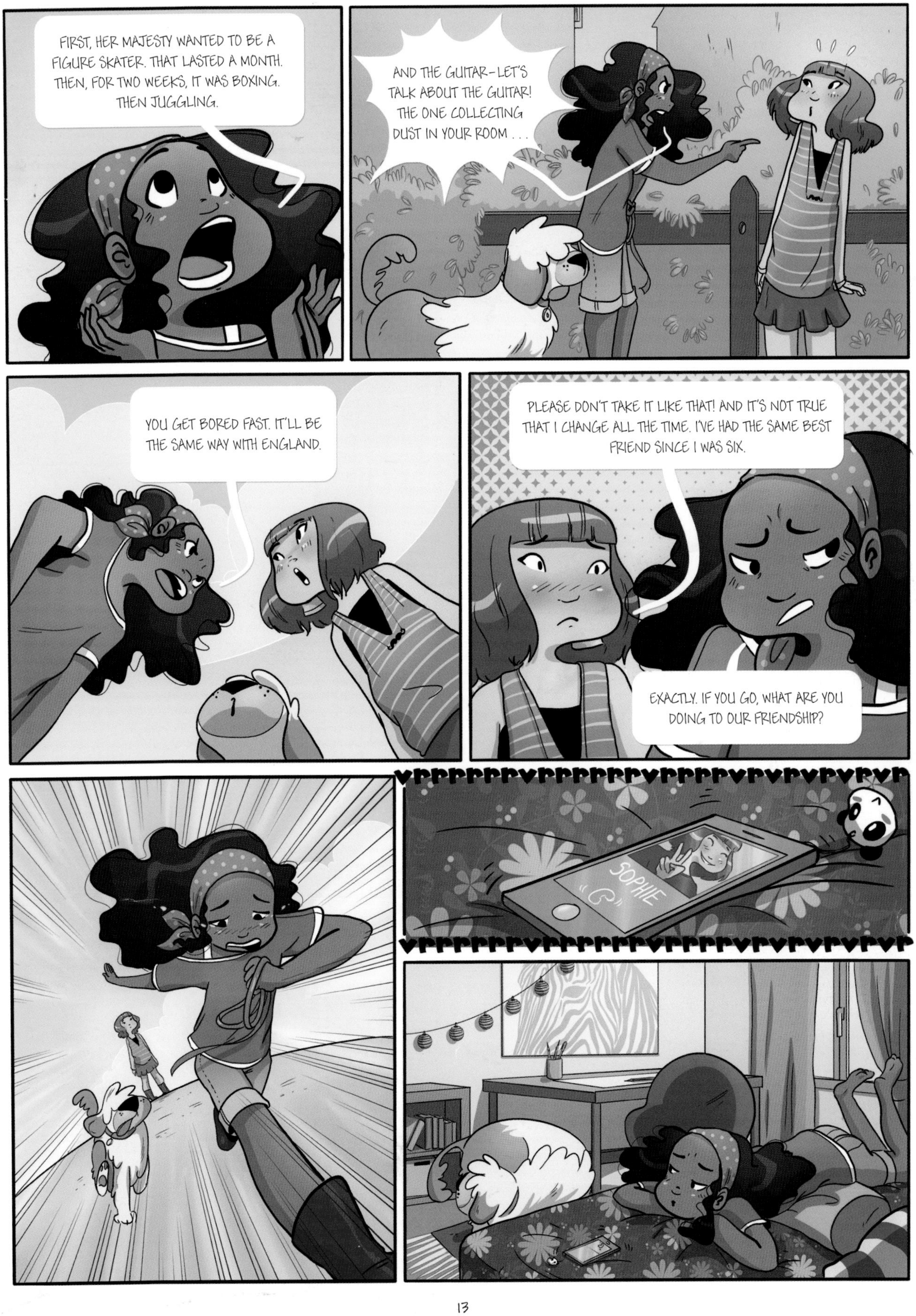
FIRST, HER MAJESTY WANTED TO BE A FIGURE SKATER. THAT LASTED A MONTH. THEN, FOR TWO WEEKS, IT WAS BOXING. THEN JUGGLING.
AND THE GUITAR–LET'S TALK ABOUT THE GUITAR! THE ONE COLLECTING DUST IN YOUR ROOM . . .
YOU GET BORED FAST. IT'LL BE THE SAME WAY WITH ENGLAND.
PLEASE DON'T TAKE IT LIKE THAT! AND IT'S NOT TRUE THAT I CHANGE ALL THE TIME. I'VE HAD THE SAME BEST FRIEND SINCE I WAS SIX.
EXACTLY. IF YOU GO, WHAT ARE YOU DOING TO OUR FRIENDSHIP?
SOPHIE

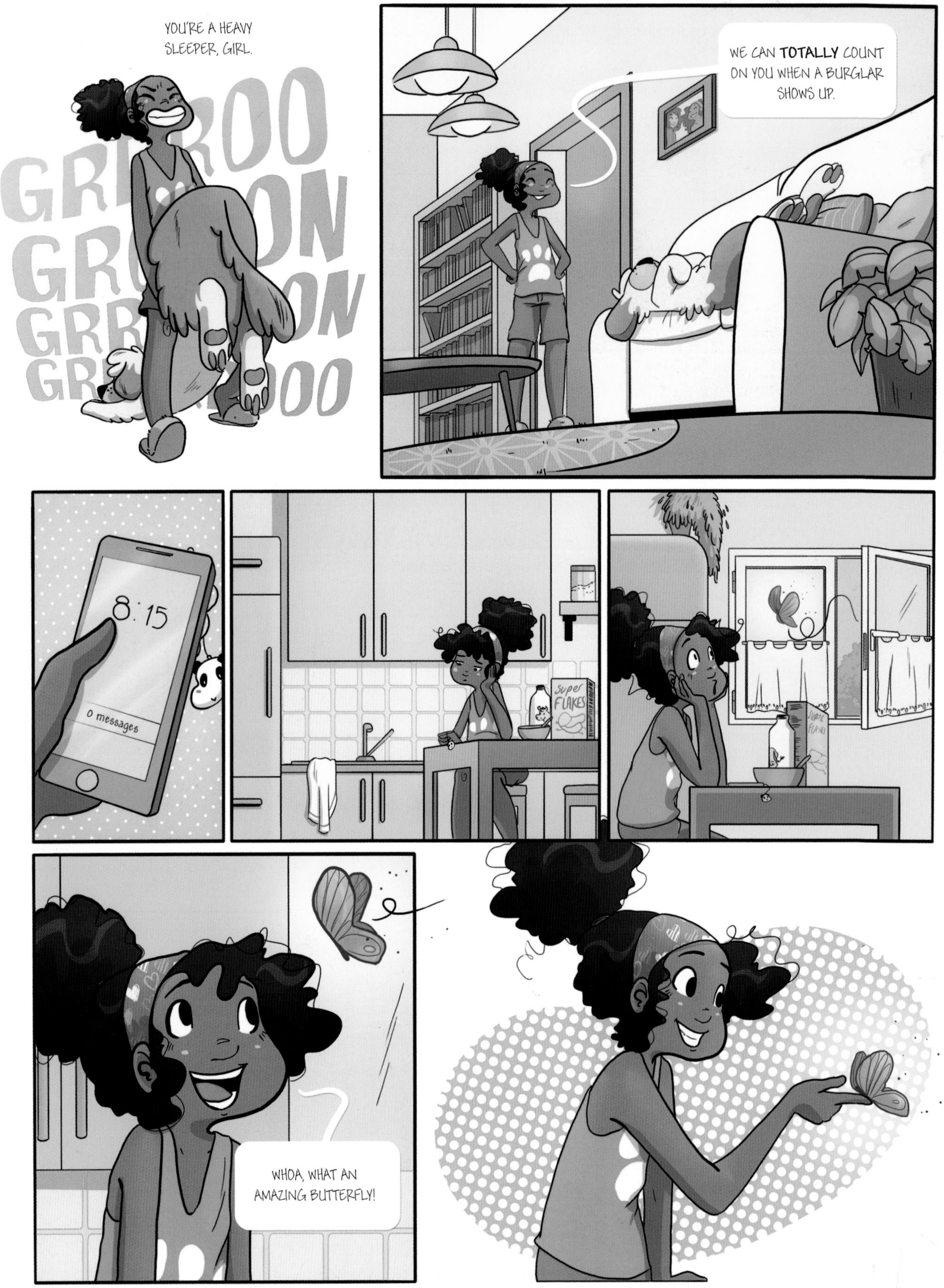
YOU'RE A HEAVY SLEEPER, GIRL.
GRRROO GRRRON GRRRON GRRROOO
WE CAN **TOTALLY** COUNT ON YOU WHEN A BURGLAR SHOWS UP.
8:15
0 messages
Super FLAKES
WHOA, WHAT AN AMAZING BUTTERFLY!

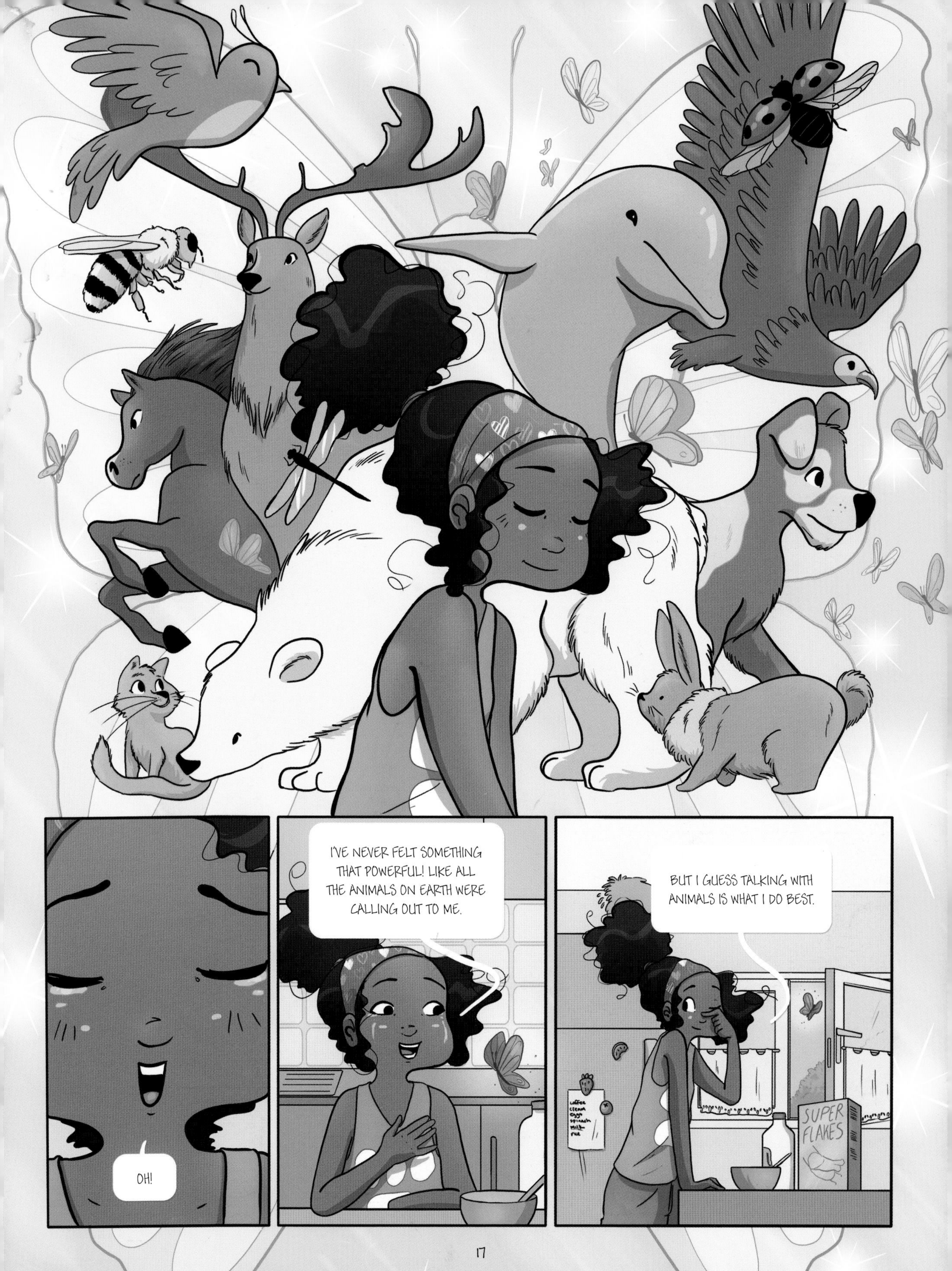
OH!
I'VE NEVER FELT SOMETHING THAT POWERFUL! LIKE ALL THE ANIMALS ON EARTH WERE CALLING OUT TO ME.
BUT I GUESS TALKING WITH ANIMALS IS WHAT I DO BEST.
SUPER FLAKES

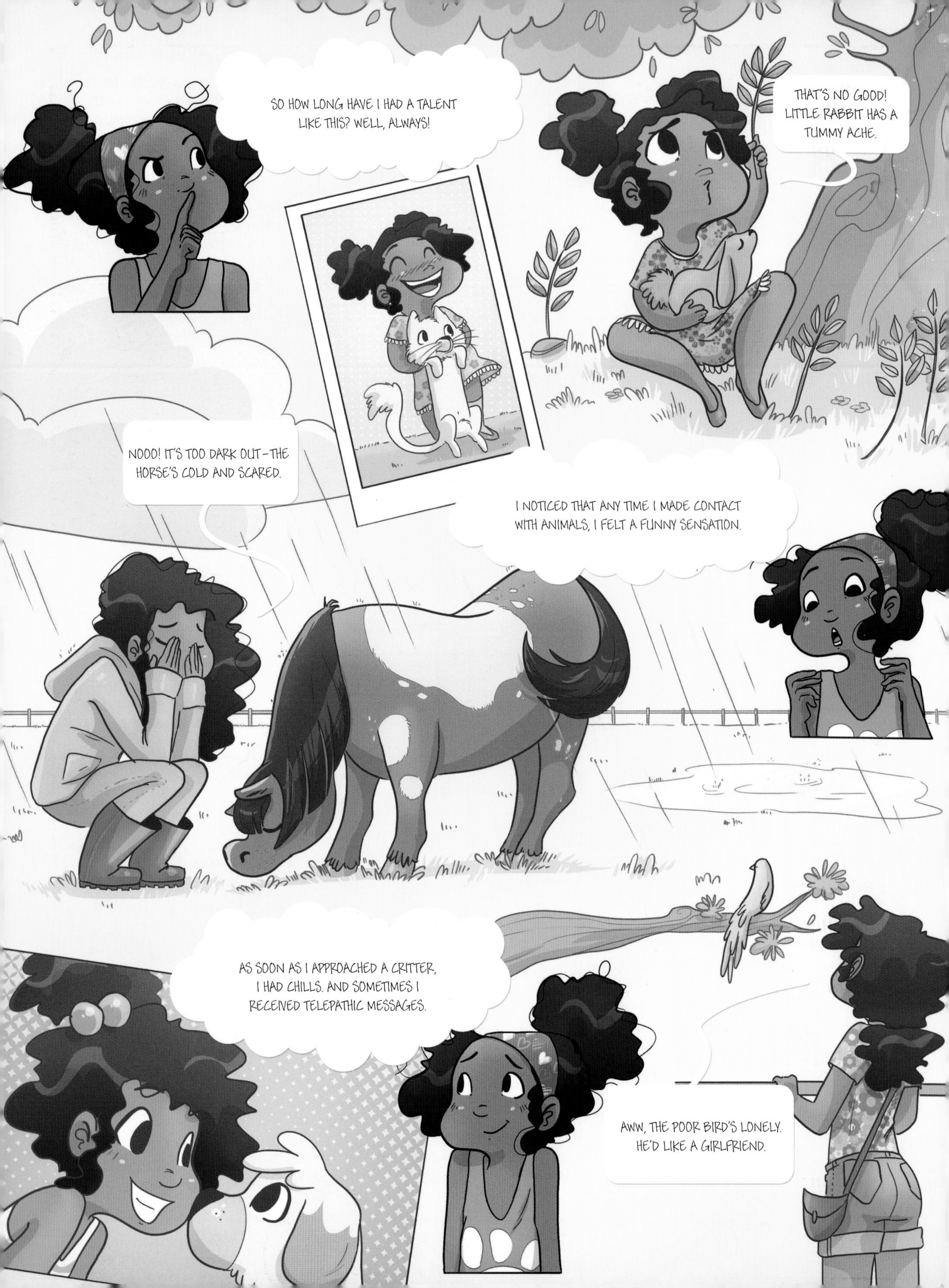
SO HOW LONG HAVE I HAD A TALENT LIKE THIS? WELL, ALWAYS!
THAT'S NO GOOD! LITTLE RABBIT HAS A TUMMY ACHE.
NOOO! IT'S TOO DARK OUT—THE HORSE'S COLD AND SCARED.
I NOTICED THAT ANY TIME I MADE CONTACT WITH ANIMALS, I FELT A FUNNY SENSATION.
AS SOON AS I APPROACHED A CRITTER, I HAD CHILLS. AND SOMETIMES I RECEIVED TELEPATHIC MESSAGES.
AWW, THE POOR BIRD'S LONELY. HE'D LIKE A GIRLFRIEND.

Mission: Titus

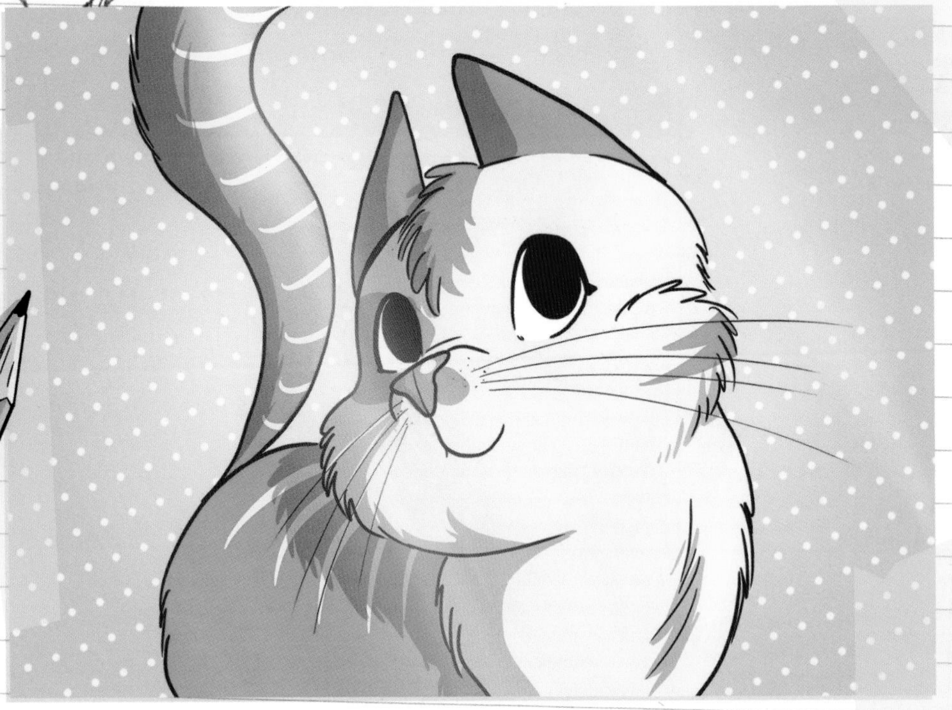

Facts of his disappearance: Serge, the owner, lives in a house with his son, Dimitri, and his girlfriend, Ariel. Titus often leaves the house to walk through their neighborhood, but he always comes back. He doesn't usually go past the street where he lives.

Serge and Dimitri discovered his disappearance on the morning of July 15. Did he disappear the previous night or earlier that morning? Nobody is sure.

Special Facts (from Dimitri)

- gentle
- picky eater
- loves to nap

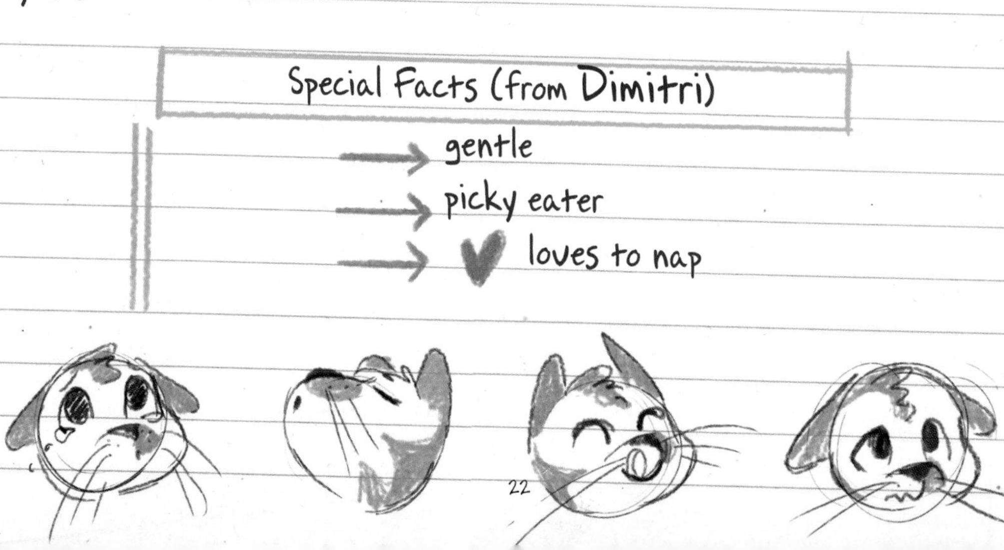

How long has the cat been in the family?

One day when they were picnicking, Serge and Dimitri found Titus in a forest. He looked lost, and he wouldn't stop meowing after Dimitri. After making sure the cat didn't belong to anybody, Serge decided to keep it. And Dimitri and Titus hardly ever left each other's side. Dimitri was three years old when they adopted Titus. Now he's five.

Dimitri was a hyperactive child. He was always restless. Results: He often got distracted, he didn't listen when he was spoken to, and he could get super giddy. But having Titus in his life was a huge change. The cat even helped him focus! THANK YOU, TITUS!!

→ Dimitri's dad called the police and the neighborhood shelters.
→ He visited all the places that Titus likes to go: their garden and the neighbors' gardens. But no neighbor had found the cat.
→ Serge has left his number with animal welfare people and at the pound.

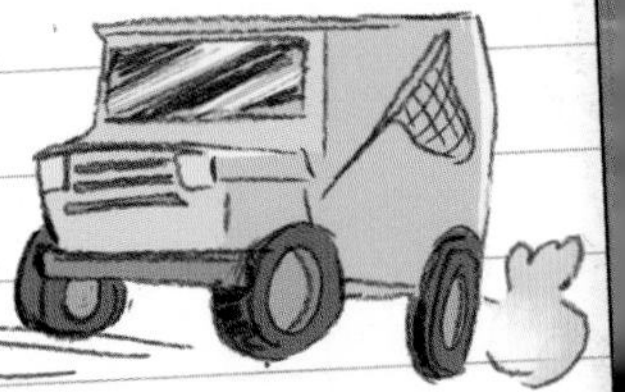

Tips I Gave Serge

→ Call city maintenance people, in case they found a crushed cat somewhere. I hope not!
→ Call services that keep registries of animals. If Titus was ever loose in the past and someone brought him to a shelter, he'd be in their files, and Serge and Dimitri might be able to trace him.

Little Forest Police Department

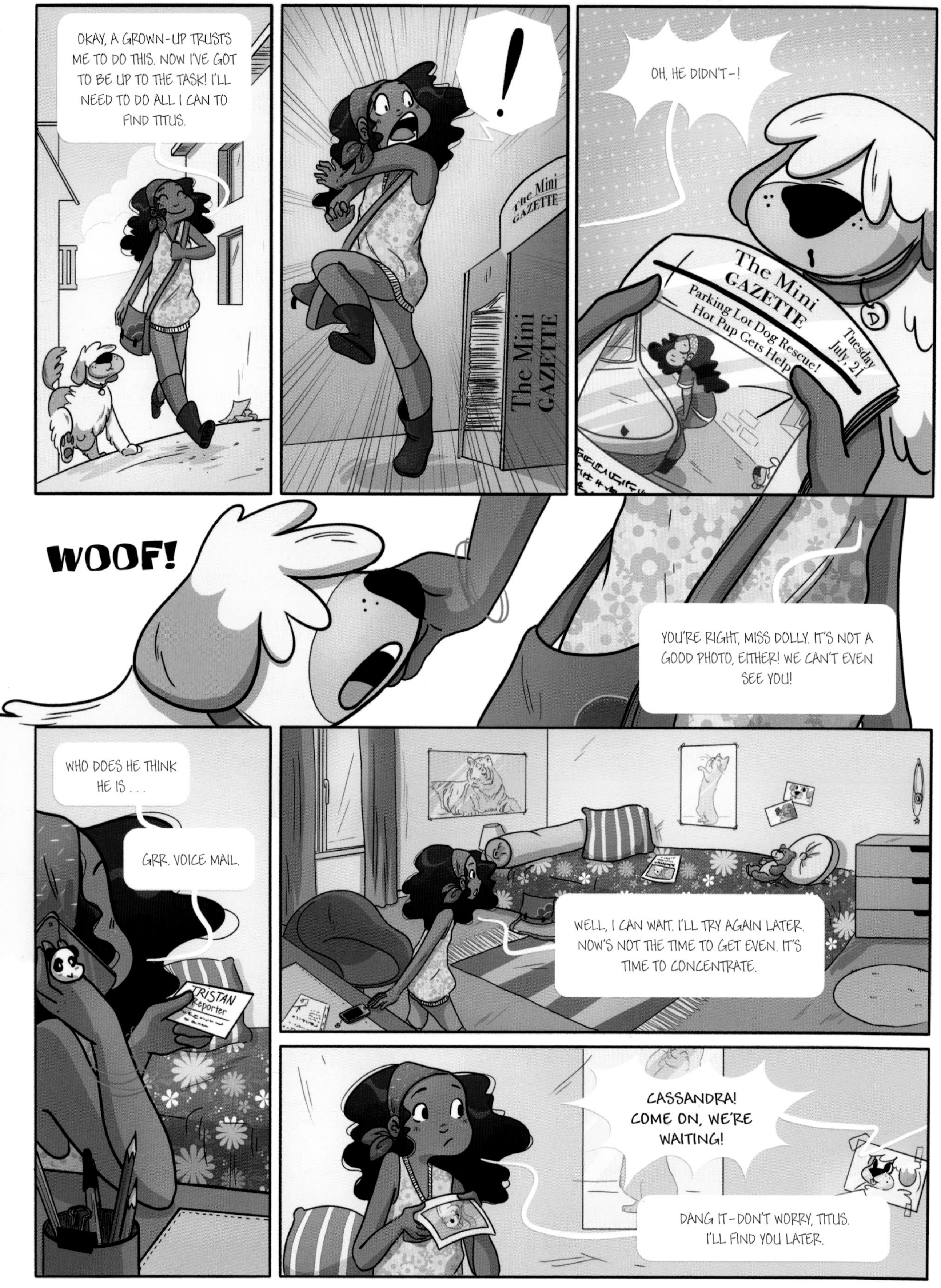
OKAY, A GROWN-UP TRUSTS ME TO DO THIS. NOW I'VE GOT TO BE UP TO THE TASK! I'LL NEED TO DO ALL I CAN TO FIND TITUS.
!
The Mini GAZETTE
The Mini GAZETTE
OH, HE DIDN'T-!
The Mini GAZETTE
Parking Lot Dog Rescue! Hot Pup Gets Help
Tuesday July, 21
WOOF!
YOU'RE RIGHT, MISS DOLLY. IT'S NOT A GOOD PHOTO, EITHER! WE CAN'T EVEN SEE YOU!
WHO DOES HE THINK HE IS . . .
GRR. VOICE MAIL.
TRISTAN Reporter
WELL, I CAN WAIT. I'LL TRY AGAIN LATER. NOW'S NOT THE TIME TO GET EVEN. IT'S TIME TO CONCENTRATE.
CASSANDRA! COME ON, WE'RE WAITING!
DANG IT-DON'T WORRY, TITUS. I'LL FIND YOU LATER.

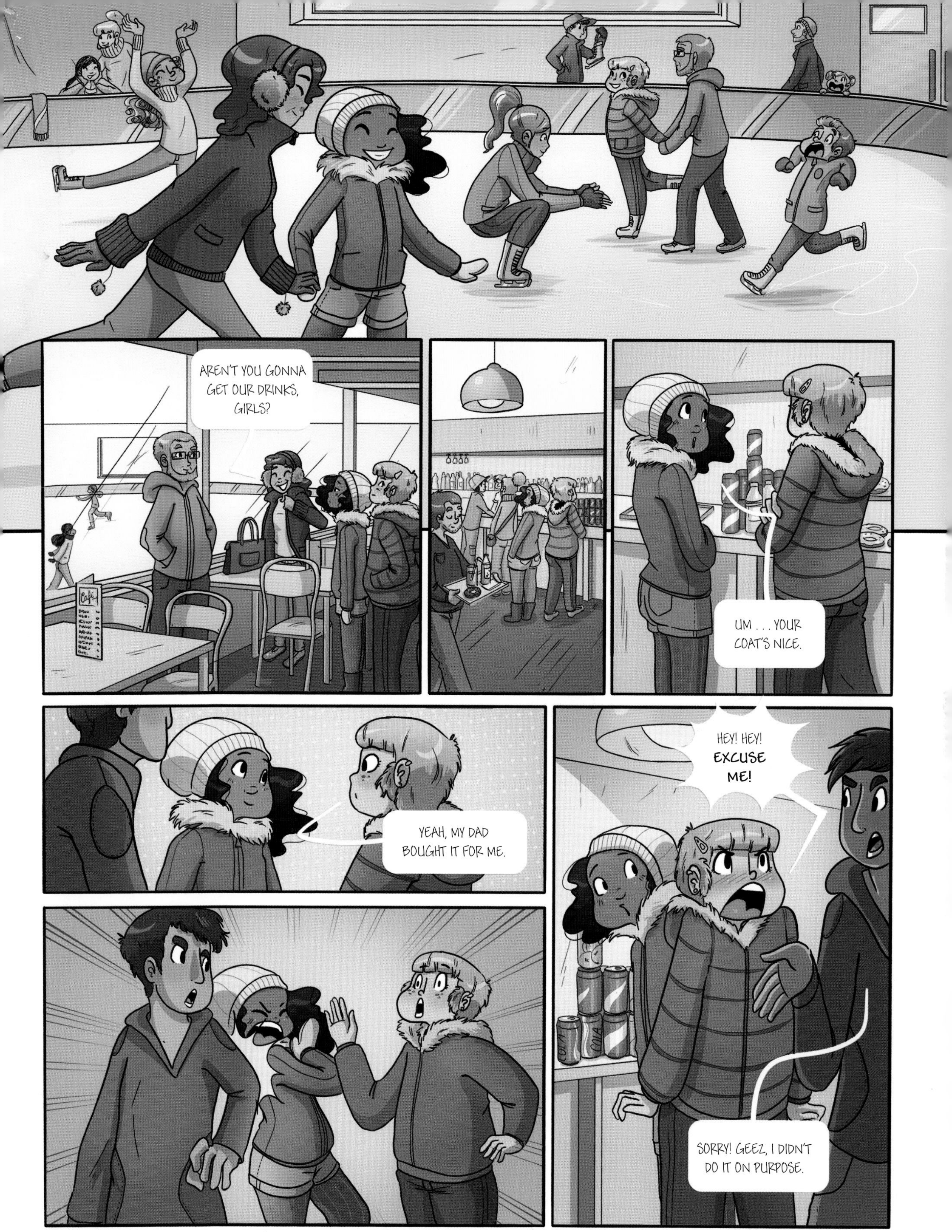
AREN'T YOU GONNA GET OUR DRINKS, GIRLS?
UM . . . YOUR COAT'S NICE.
YEAH, MY DAD BOUGHT IT FOR ME.
HEY! HEY! EXCUSE ME!
SORRY! GEEZ, I DIDN'T DO IT ON PURPOSE.

27

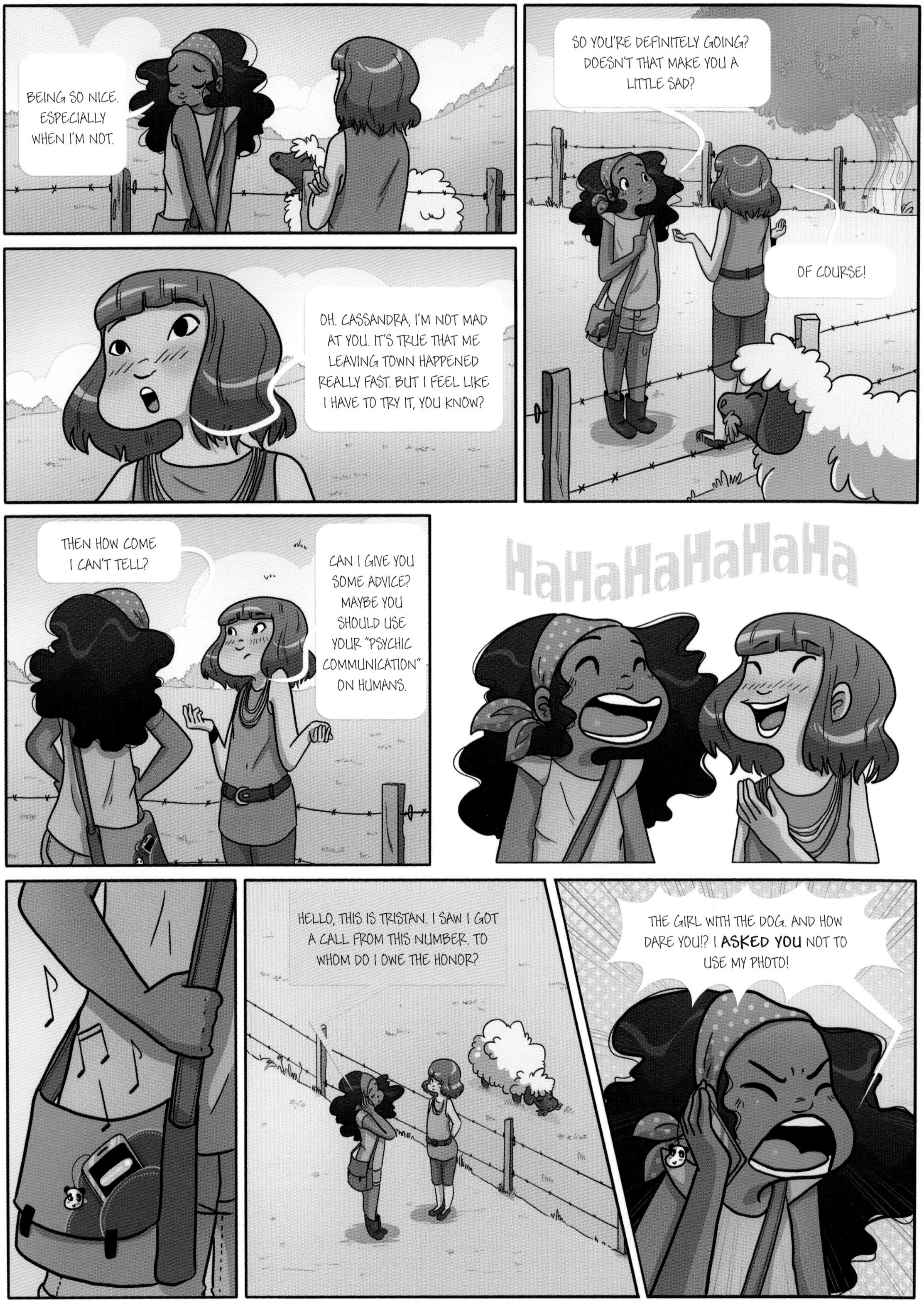
BEING SO NICE. ESPECIALLY WHEN I'M NOT.
SO YOU'RE DEFINITELY GOING? DOESN'T THAT MAKE YOU A LITTLE SAD?
OF COURSE!
OH. CASSANDRA, I'M NOT MAD AT YOU. IT'S TRUE THAT ME LEAVING TOWN HAPPENED REALLY FAST. BUT I FEEL LIKE I HAVE TO TRY IT, YOU KNOW?
THEN HOW COME I CAN'T TELL?
CAN I GIVE YOU SOME ADVICE? MAYBE YOU SHOULD USE YOUR "PSYCHIC COMMUNICATION" ON HUMANS.
HaHaHaHaHaHa
HELLO, THIS IS TRISTAN. I SAW I GOT A CALL FROM THIS NUMBER. TO WHOM DO I OWE THE HONOR?
THE GIRL WITH THE DOG. AND HOW DARE YOU!? I ASKED YOU NOT TO USE MY PHOTO!

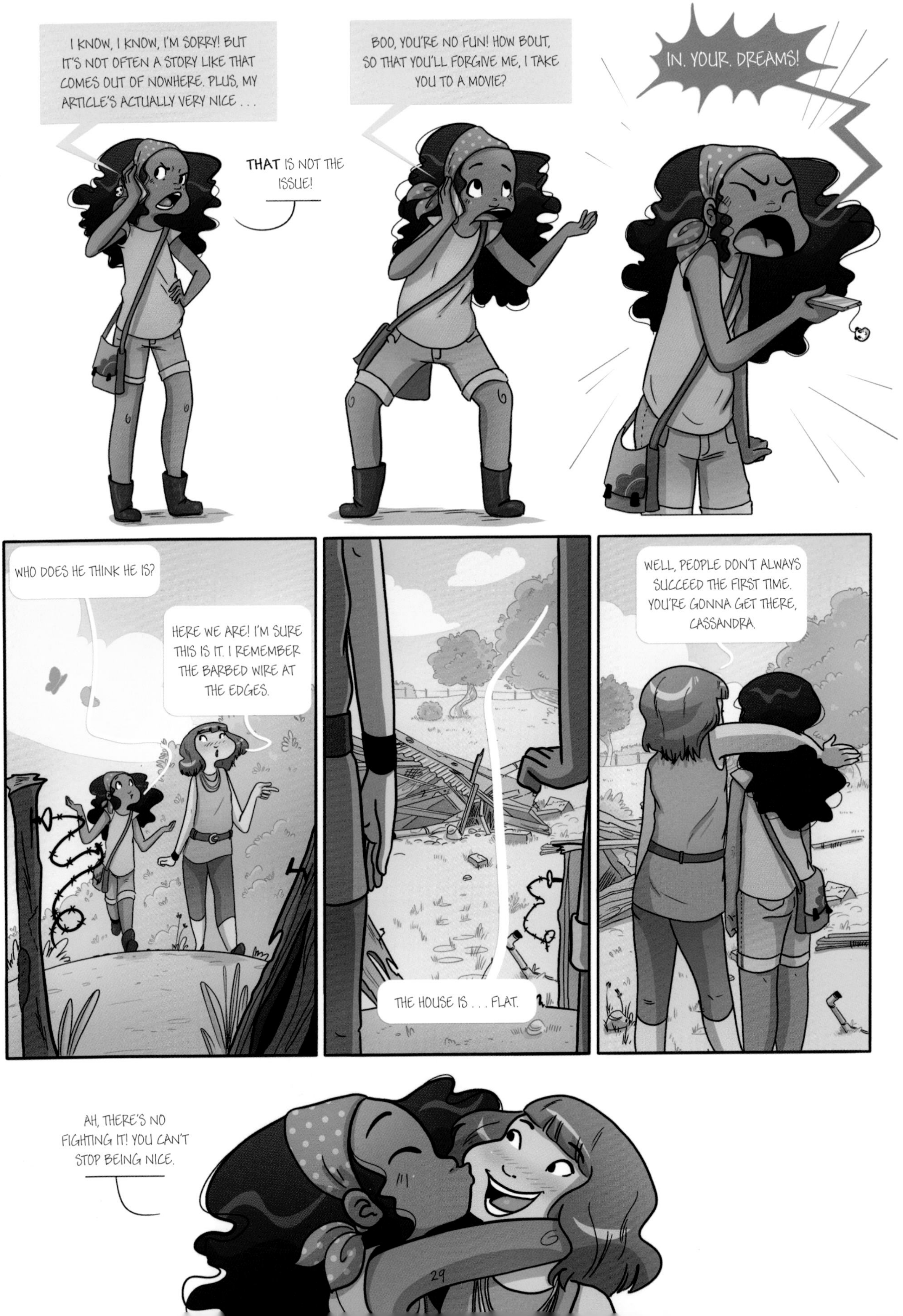

I KNOW, I KNOW, I'M SORRY! BUT IT'S NOT OFTEN A STORY LIKE THAT COMES OUT OF NOWHERE. PLUS, MY ARTICLE'S ACTUALLY VERY NICE . . .
THAT IS NOT THE ISSUE!
BOO, YOU'RE NO FUN! HOW BOUT, SO THAT YOU'LL FORGIVE ME, I TAKE YOU TO A MOVIE?
IN. YOUR. DREAMS!
WHO DOES HE THINK HE IS?
HERE WE ARE! I'M SURE THIS IS IT. I REMEMBER THE BARBED WIRE AT THE EDGES.
THE HOUSE IS . . . FLAT.
WELL, PEOPLE DON'T ALWAYS SUCCEED THE FIRST TIME. YOU'RE GONNA GET THERE, CASSANDRA.
AH, THERE'S NO FIGHTING IT! YOU CAN'T STOP BEING NICE.

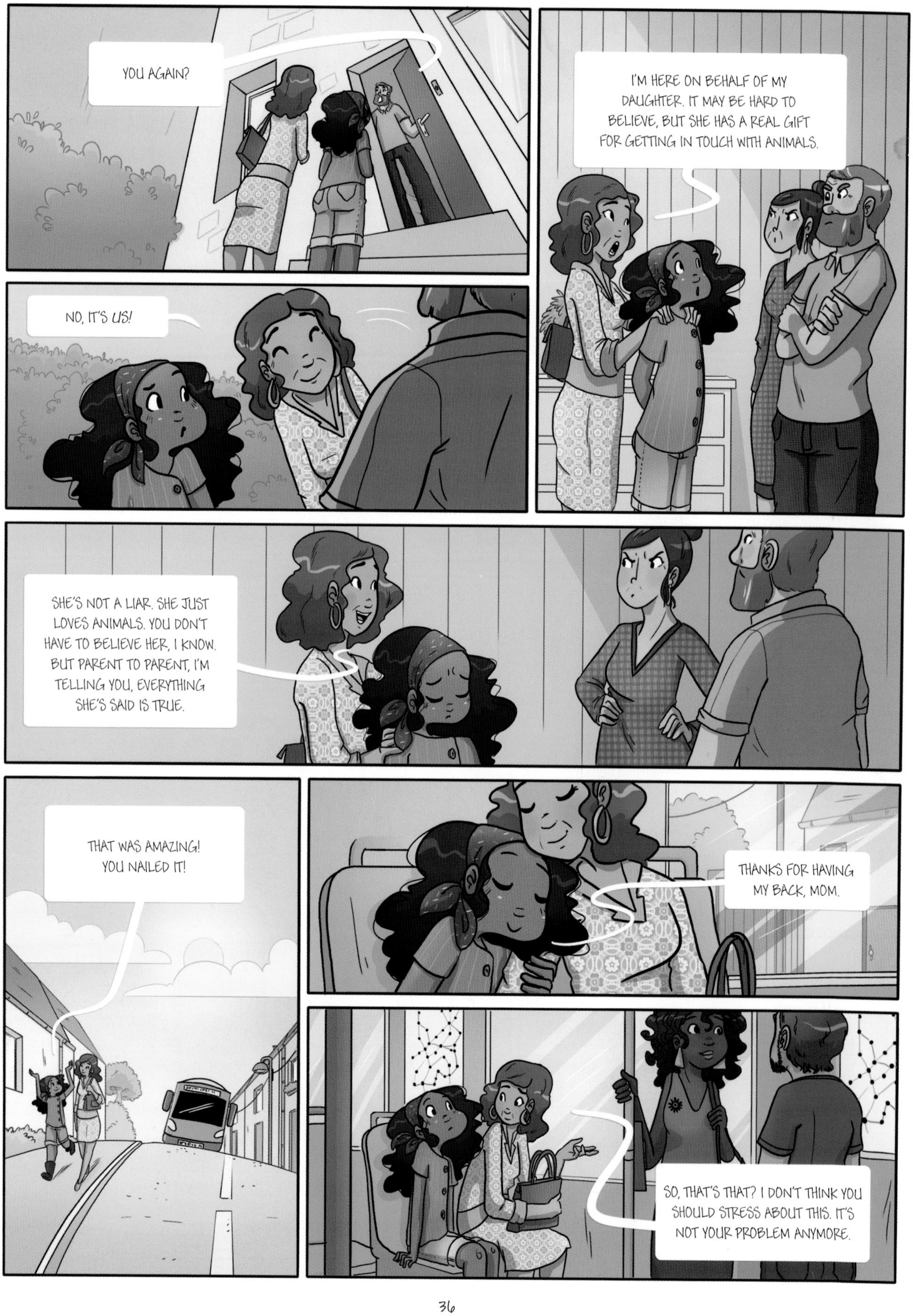
YOU AGAIN?
I'M HERE ON BEHALF OF MY DAUGHTER. IT MAY BE HARD TO BELIEVE, BUT SHE HAS A REAL GIFT FOR GETTING IN TOUCH WITH ANIMALS.
NO, IT'S *US*!
SHE'S NOT A LIAR. SHE JUST LOVES ANIMALS. YOU DON'T HAVE TO BELIEVE HER, I KNOW. BUT PARENT TO PARENT, I'M TELLING YOU, EVERYTHING SHE'S SAID IS TRUE.
THAT WAS AMAZING! YOU NAILED IT!
THANKS FOR HAVING MY BACK, MOM.
SO, THAT'S THAT? I DON'T THINK YOU SHOULD STRESS ABOUT THIS. IT'S NOT YOUR PROBLEM ANYMORE.

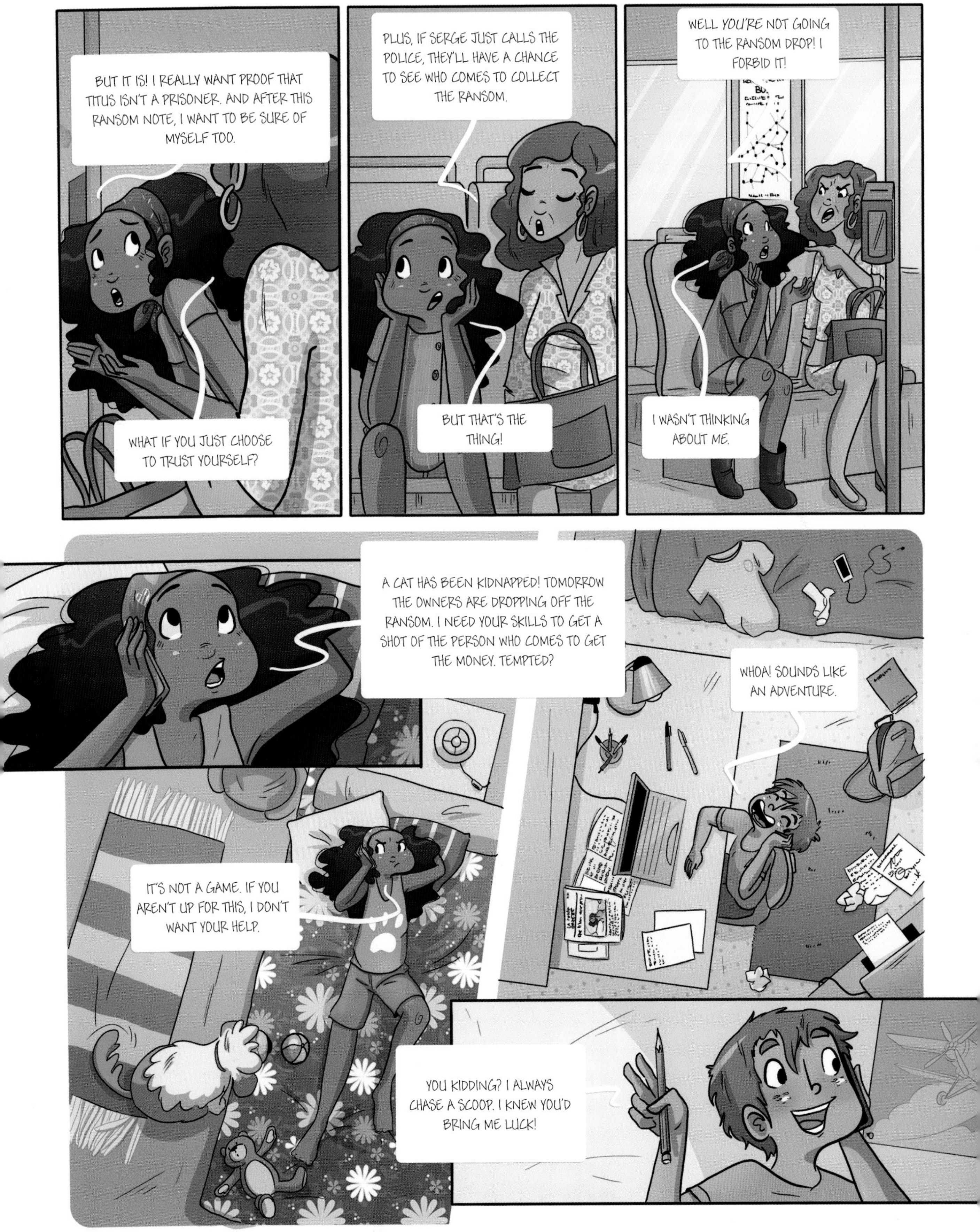
BUT IT IS! I REALLY WANT PROOF THAT TITUS ISN'T A PRISONER. AND AFTER THIS RANSOM NOTE, I WANT TO BE SURE OF MYSELF TOO.
WHAT IF YOU JUST CHOOSE TO TRUST YOURSELF?
PLUS, IF SERGE JUST CALLS THE POLICE, THEY'LL HAVE A CHANCE TO SEE WHO COMES TO COLLECT THE RANSOM.
BUT THAT'S THE THING!
WELL YOU'RE NOT GOING TO THE RANSOM DROP! I FORBID IT!
I WASN'T THINKING ABOUT ME.
A CAT HAS BEEN KIDNAPPED! TOMORROW THE OWNERS ARE DROPPING OFF THE RANSOM. I NEED YOUR SKILLS TO GET A SHOT OF THE PERSON WHO COMES TO GET THE MONEY. TEMPTED?
WHOA! SOUNDS LIKE AN ADVENTURE.
IT'S NOT A GAME. IF YOU AREN'T UP FOR THIS, I DON'T WANT YOUR HELP.
YOU KIDDING? I ALWAYS CHASE A SCOOP. I KNEW YOU'D BRING ME LUCK!

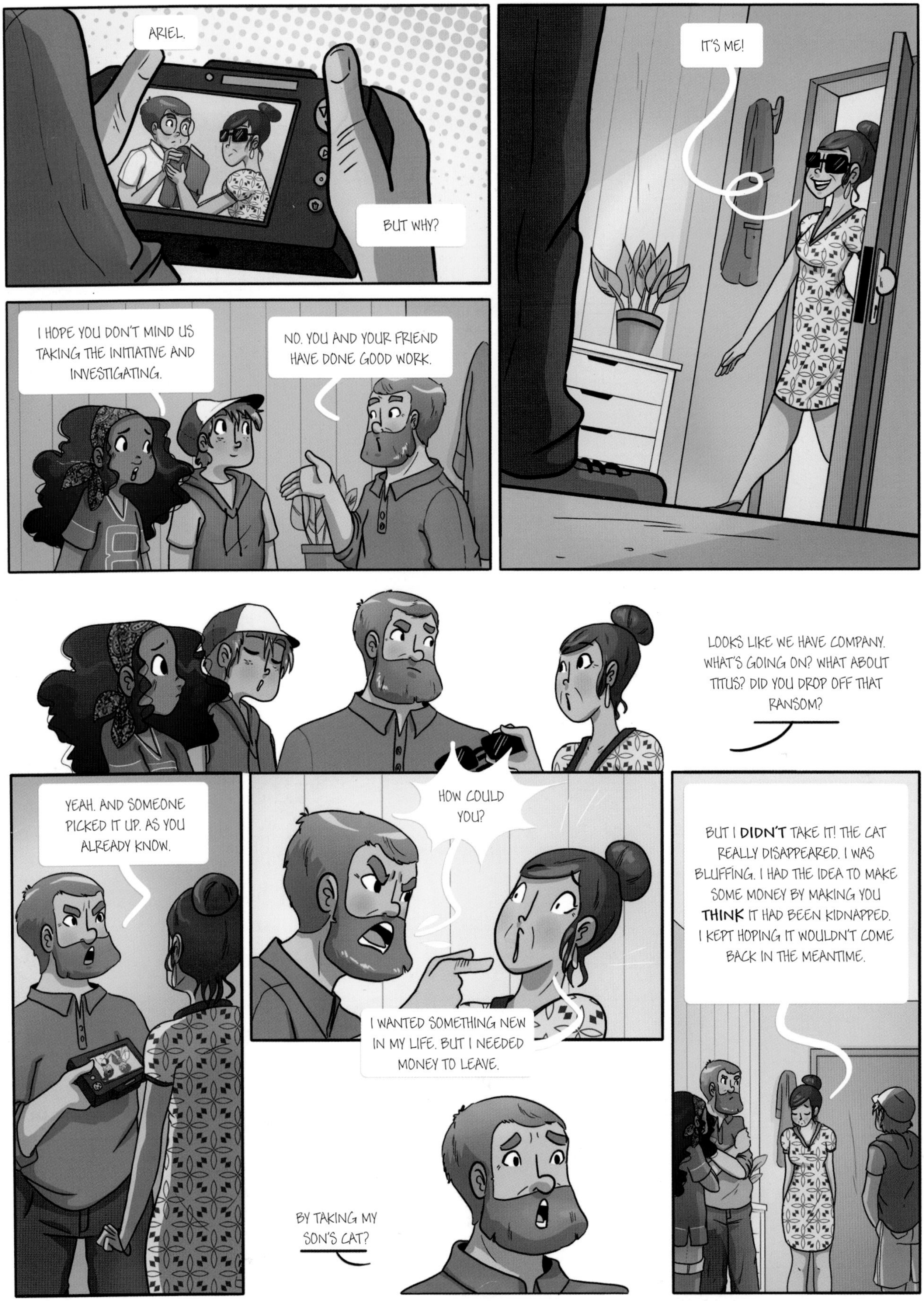
ARIEL.
BUT WHY?
IT'S ME!
I HOPE YOU DON'T MIND US TAKING THE INITIATIVE AND INVESTIGATING.
NO. YOU AND YOUR FRIEND HAVE DONE GOOD WORK.
LOOKS LIKE WE HAVE COMPANY. WHAT'S GOING ON? WHAT ABOUT TITUS? DID YOU DROP OFF THAT RANSOM?
YEAH. AND SOMEONE PICKED IT UP. AS YOU ALREADY KNOW.
HOW COULD YOU?
I WANTED SOMETHING NEW IN MY LIFE. BUT I NEEDED MONEY TO LEAVE.
BY TAKING MY SON'S CAT?
BUT I **DIDN'T** TAKE IT! THE CAT REALLY DISAPPEARED. I WAS BLUFFING. I HAD THE IDEA TO MAKE SOME MONEY BY MAKING YOU **THINK** IT HAD BEEN KIDNAPPED. I KEPT HOPING IT WOULDN'T COME BACK IN THE MEANTIME.

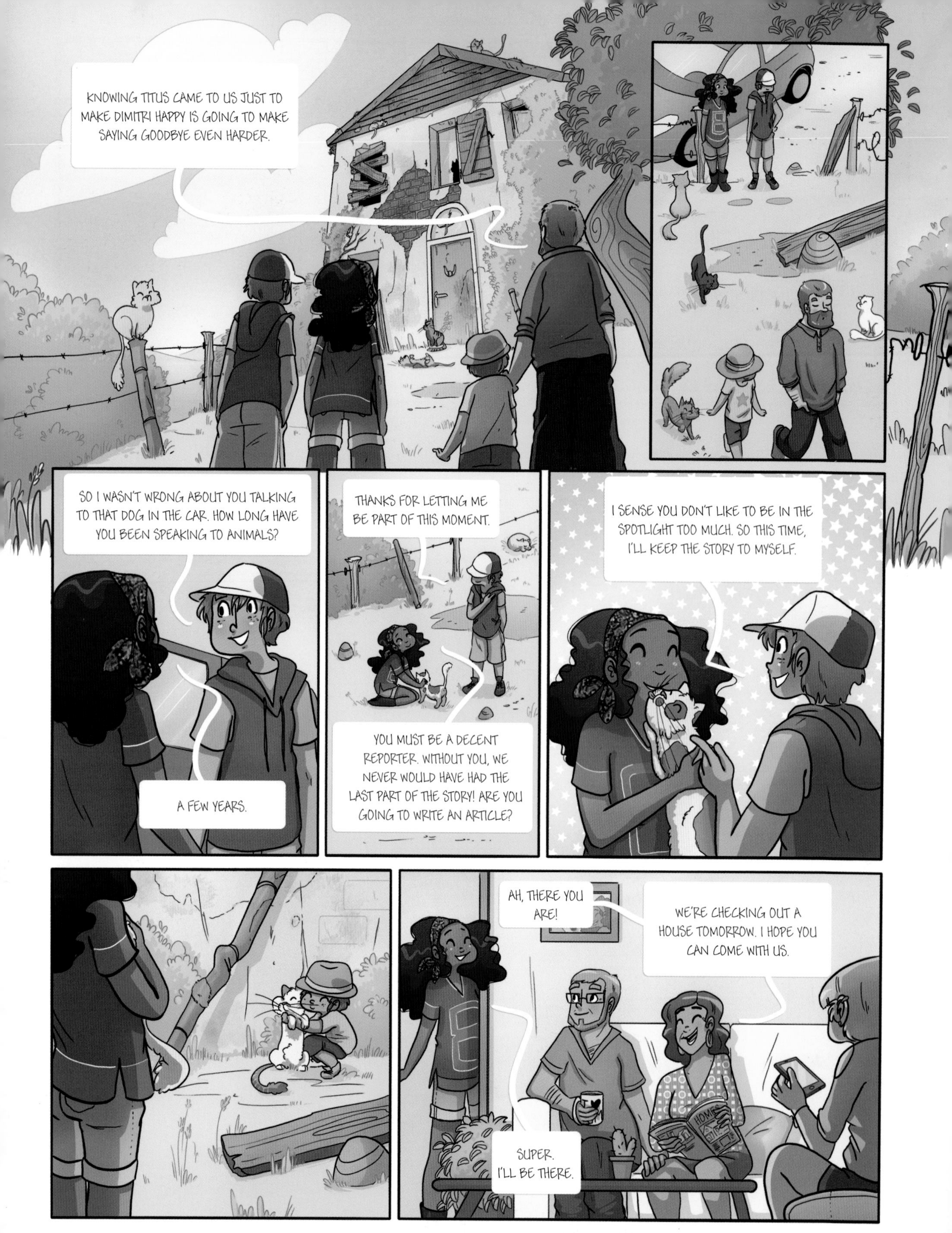
KNOWING TITUS CAME TO US JUST TO MAKE DIMITRI HAPPY IS GOING TO MAKE SAYING GOODBYE EVEN HARDER.
SO I WASN'T WRONG ABOUT YOU TALKING TO THAT DOG IN THE CAR. HOW LONG HAVE YOU BEEN SPEAKING TO ANIMALS?
A FEW YEARS.
THANKS FOR LETTING ME BE PART OF THIS MOMENT.
YOU MUST BE A DECENT REPORTER. WITHOUT YOU, WE NEVER WOULD HAVE HAD THE LAST PART OF THE STORY! ARE YOU GOING TO WRITE AN ARTICLE?
I SENSE YOU DON'T LIKE TO BE IN THE SPOTLIGHT TOO MUCH. SO THIS TIME, I'LL KEEP THE STORY TO MYSELF.
AH, THERE YOU ARE!
WE'RE CHECKING OUT A HOUSE TOMORROW. I HOPE YOU CAN COME WITH US.
SUPER. I'LL BE THERE.

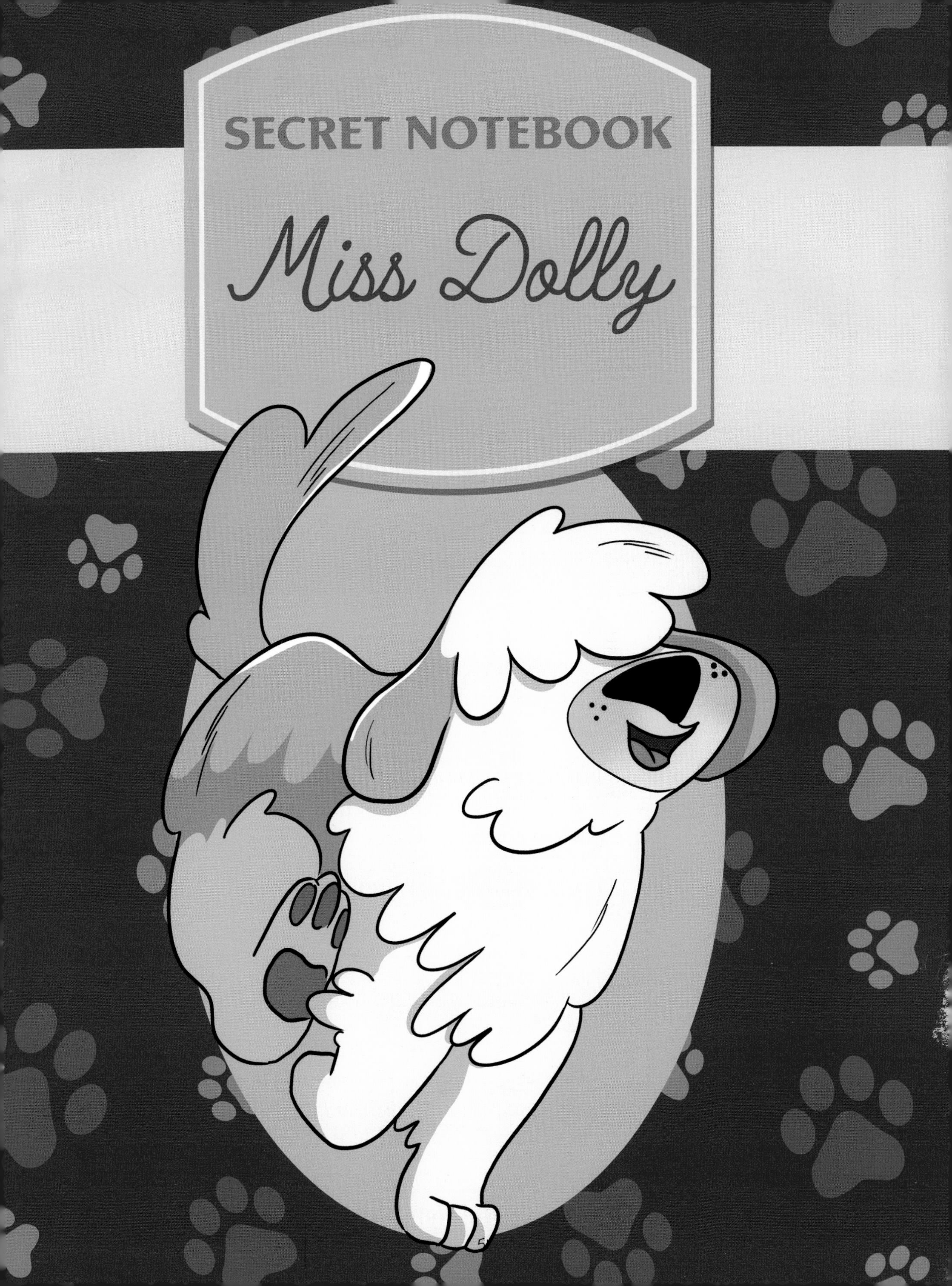
SECRET NOTEBOOK
Miss Dolly

Memories, memories . . .

HOW I MET MISS DOLLY:

When I turned ten, Mom surprised me by taking me to a shelter so we could adopt a dog. I went crazy with joy! I'd been waiting for this day for so long. It had always been my dream to have a dog!

* * *

I couldn't wait to meet the pooch who was going to be my new friend. While almost all the puppies greeted me with some happy woofs, Miss Dolly was the only one to completely ignore me. She kept lying in her corner, folded in on herself, sighing long sighs. She looked so sad and miserable that my sensitive heart couldn't resist. THAT'S HOW SHE WON ME OVER, HANDS DOWN!

Who's this?

Miss Dolly has a big bobtail.

She's an English shepherd.

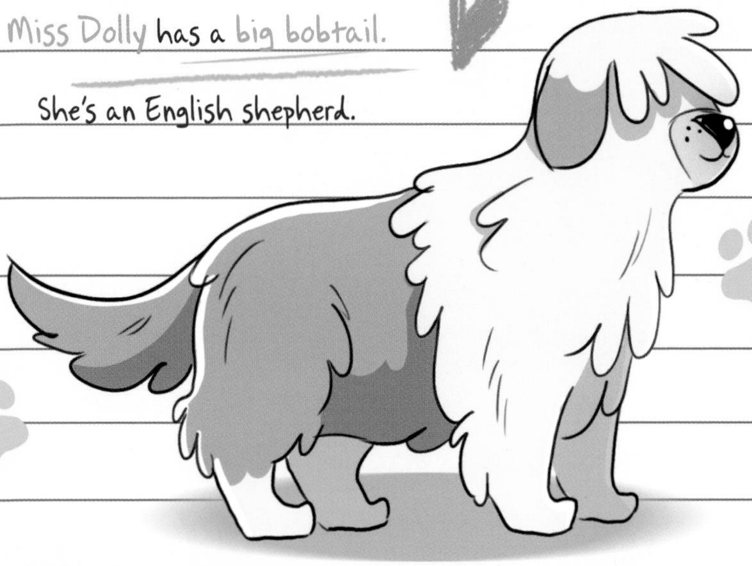

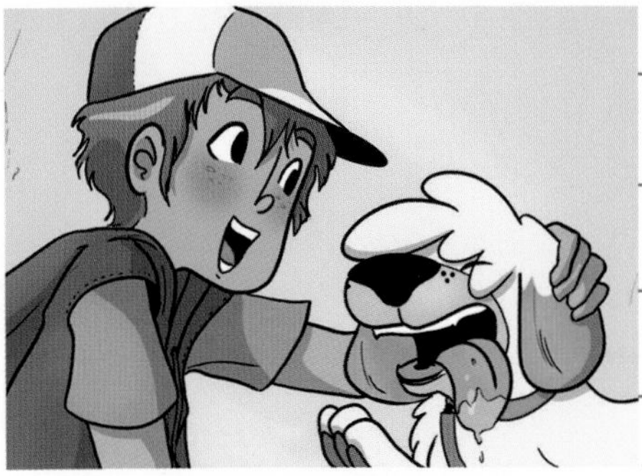

This bobtailed shepherd is very sociable. She gets along with everyone.

She's a big friend of the kids!

She's also a good sport whenever I put her hair up.

No joke!

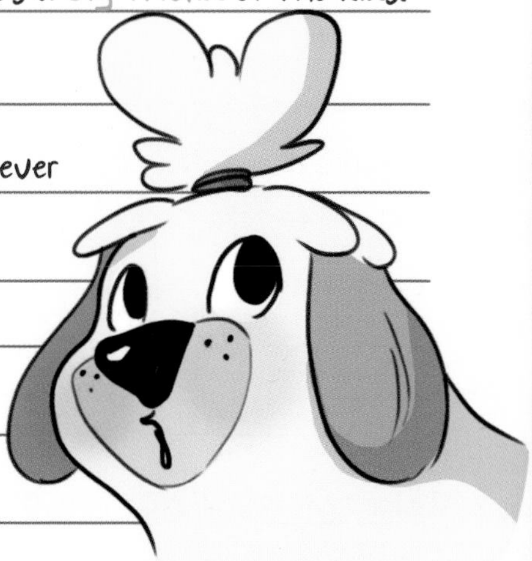

Her coat requires a lot of maintenance and grooming.

Decoding Miss Dolly's behavior

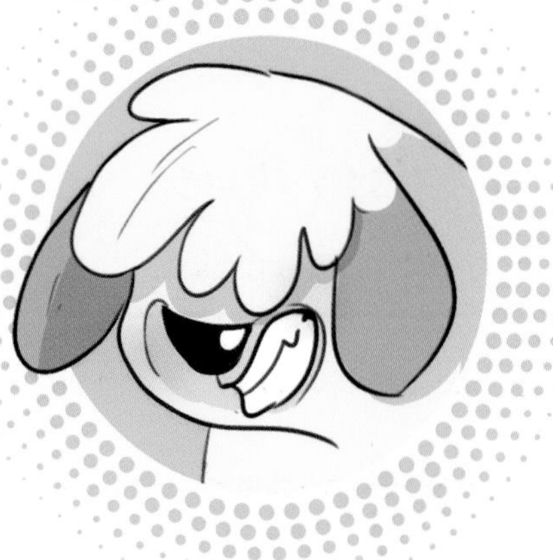

WARNING!

This is the look of a dog that has made a big mistake. Better act fast!

This look says you have something Miss Dolly wants, like ice cream or a hot dog. Ignore it!

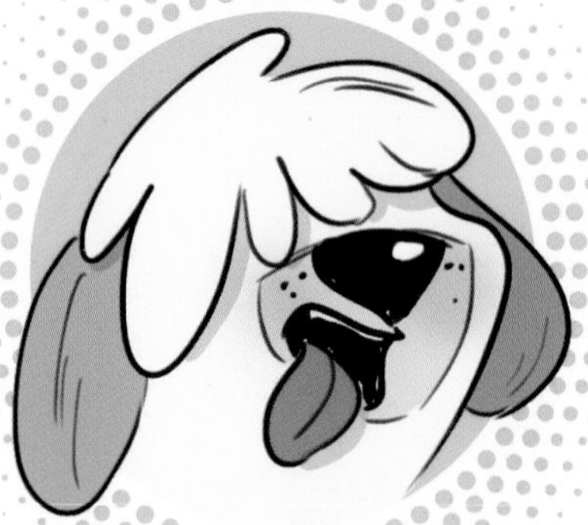

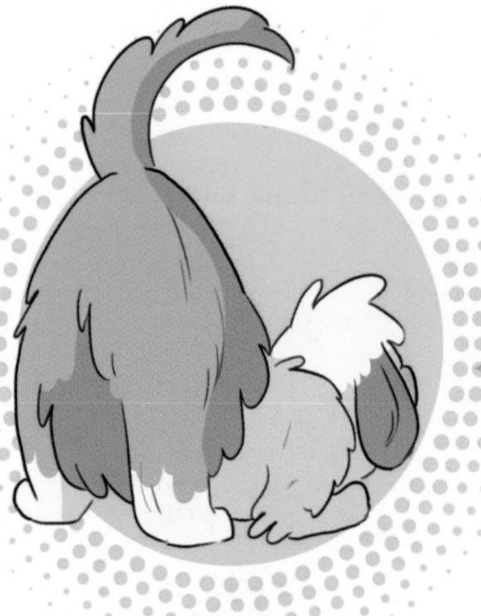

This means she will do anything for a piece of sausage, even busting out her butt-wiggling dance to get your attention!

When a dog sleeps on its side, that means it feels cozy in its space. She can relax and sleep because she's comfortable. Thank you, my Dolly!

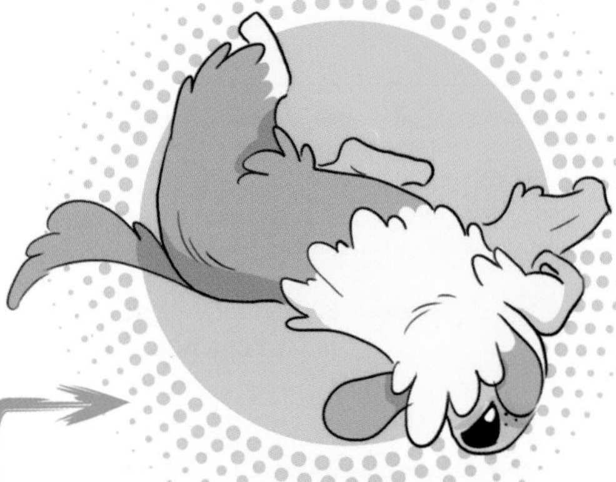

Miss Dolly, the Queen of Goofiness!

This dog lives in the moment. If I catch her doing something naughty, I scold her. But if I'm not sure when the naughtiness happened, I let her be. Miss Dolly wouldn't understand why I'm scolding her because she already would have forgotten what she did.

When Miss Dolly was a puppy, sometimes she would pee inside. To show her little by little what was good and what was bad, if I took her out and she did her business, I'd reward her with a little treat. Miss Dolly understood really quickly:

peeing inside = we have a problem

peeing outside = you get a snack

About the Author

Isabelle Bottier

Isabelle Bottier is a writer based in Ile-de-France, France. She made her debut writing for French television and quickly began to write on several animated series. She also uses her imagination to create comics for young readers.

About the Artist

Hélène Canac

Hélène Canac lives in the sanctuary of comics, Angoulême, France. She has studied graphic design, publishing, and advertising, and she worked in animation after her time as a student. She also works in youth illustration, providing art for novels, games, notebooks . . . and, most recently, comics!

Coming soon:
the second Cassandra:
Animal Psychic graphic novel,
Out on a Limb!